Those Other People

Those Other People

ALICE CHILDRESS

G. P. Putnam's Sons
New York

Published simultaneously
in Canada. Printed in the United States of America
Book design by Gunta Alexander
First impression

Library of Congress Cataloging-in-Publication Data
Childress, Alice. Those other people / Alice Childress. p. cm.
Summary: Bigotry surfaces at Minitown High when a popular male
teacher sexually assaults a delinquent fifteen-year-old girl and
the only witnesses are a black boy and a gay student teacher.
ISBN 0-399-21510-7
[1. Prejudices—Fiction. 2. Rape—Fiction. 3. Homosexuality—Fiction.
4. Afro-Americans—Fiction. 5. High schools—Fiction. 6. Schools—
Fiction.]
I. Title. PZ7.C4412Th 1988 [Fic]—dc19 88-10309 CIP AC

To my husband

NATHAN WOODARD

for his belief and encouragement

Contents

Those Other People

1 *Jonathan Barnett*

IT IS THE NIGHT BEFORE THE MINITOWN HIGH school board meeting. I sure don't want to be there. I'm seventeen years old, a temporary computer instructor, and I've been running away from one thing or another for too long. From my parents' home in a New York State suburb to second and third places in New York City, then back home to Marsley Falls—now living in Minitown. I'm in my studio apartment, sitting on the floor in front of a fireplace with imitation gas logs made of stone composition stuff. There's a handle on one side. Turn it and gas comes out the same as with the kitchen stove, except there's no pilot. You have to strike a match. I'm alone except for a cat named Lataweeze. Lat rhymes with cat. She's stretched out on a raggedy floor pillow. Lataweeze is quality alley. Looks at me like she's trying to read my mind.

Now I'm thinking back to about three months ago, a night in New York City's Greenwich Village. I had entered the apartment just in time to hear Harp, my twenty-two-year-old roommate, loud-mouthing me over the phone. "Jonathan Barnett is gay, a fruit. Jon-baby's limp in the wrist. In your terms, a homosexual. He's too chicken to emerge from his dark secret closet, so I'm giving him this coming-out announcement. Because I'm his lover, that's why, the lover who loves everything about him except his cowardice."

A mean streak surfaces when Harper Mead gets into too much beer or wine. I thought he was blasting me to his buddy Charlie, another gay guy who pesters people about coming out. I grabbed the phone and gave the listening ear a shrill whistle and yelled "Drop dead!" There was a pause. A dull voice whispered, "Son, this is Dad. I just took the phone from your mother. Is this a bad joke?"

My stomach did a fast fall on a down elevator. Then I lied. "Dad, it is a joke. I'm sorry. We were kidding around over a couple of beers, you know? I thought you were some dumb guy on the other end."

Harp cut in from the kitchen extension. "It's no joke, Mr. Barnett. Your son is what I said and so am I. We're a pair. A couple. I'm into teaching him something about honesty."

Dad didn't answer him. "Jonathan," he said, "I thought you were living with your Aunt Rita. Would you care to come home and talk about this?" He waited.

"Yeah, sure, Dad. Anyway, I planned to be up this weekend."

His voice lifted, clear and steady. "We're looking forward to seeing you." He ignored Harp. My father has style—and a bad heart.

After that night I didn't want to go on sharing Harp's apartment—or to move back in with my parents.

I think back to the day my cousin Betty graduated from college in New England. We went up to celebrate and check out the surrounding territory for me. There were signs and posters all over campus. Sexual stuff. Gay rights discussion! Lesbians united. Bisexual society. Signs, signs and more signs. Posters on walls, tacked to bus-stop shelters, on bulletin boards, everywhere. My folks didn't seem to notice. I strolled away from them to collect my shook-up thoughts. I realized I was in no way ready for public discussions on sexual preferences. A big, lumbering heavyset guy walked up to me like he was an old friend. He shoved a leaflet in my hand and said, "Make the gay rights meeting tonight. We want our own dorm." That did it. Finalized my decision to delay college.

Being gay was slowly becoming uncomfortable. I had thought college would be an out, a way to get away from home ground. A place to do a little private thinking. But I wasn't ready to join any big-mouth crowd. Gay rights. Why the hell do people form organizations about every damn thing? I had to get away or get ready for a straitjacket.

One night I woke up talking in my sleep, hearing my own words, "Let me out, leave me alone." The next day I hinted to my folks about being gay. They never heard me. Just changed the subject like nothing had been said. I had to get away from home. Leave or else. I told them I wasn't ready for college. They sure didn't rush to accept that. I stood pat for two weeks. And then they sent me to a shrink. He halfway guessed me out and backed me up. I'd gone for his help at Mom's insistence. I knew my problem. How does the odd one fit in? Who should I hurt, myself or others? Not hurting anyone was what I wanted. Just to be free to find out how to be who I am.

Dad tried to change my mind. "No, son, don't put off your education, you're a good student. If you were physically or mentally ill I could see it. But there's no good reason. If you want work experience find a college with a work program."

That was not what I needed. "I want out, Dad, to be alone to think, to be away from home."

"Son, college is away from home."

"Dad, I'll be ready to go in another year."

"Is it your girl?"

"My girl?"

"Yes, Fern."

"No."

"She seems to care more than you are able to return."

"Maybe she does. But I do care about her a lot."

"Running away is no solution. A clean break won't hurt. You're both too young to be overly serious. If you must run, go off to school, continue your education, make space and take time in a constructive way."

"Dad, some part of myself belongs to me. Remember? You taught me that."

"You'll lose a whole year."

"I'll make it up."

"Yes, we know you will. Where do you want to go?"

"New York City. Maybe I can bunk with Aunt Rita

and get lost in the crowd. Find a job. I can come back home some weekends."

"Your mother and I don't think her baby sister Rita is very responsible. She's too young to look out for a grown boy. At thirty-seven she's not as mature as she ought to be."

"Dad, I'm seventeen. Almost of age to legally take off and walk away. Then I'll have the $3,000 Grandpa left me. I'm trying not to run away."

"Okay, Jonathan, you win. If times get tough, call home. Remember, it's no disgrace to change your mind and $3,000 is not as much as you think when you start paying your own way. What kind of job do you hope to get?"

"Anything. I don't know yet."

"Well, son, remember you do have a home."

"Thanks, Dad."

"We'll ask Rita if she can take you in."

The sound of Mom's key in the door brought our conversation to an end. They exchanged looks, and her smile faded. I realized she had gone "visiting" for a while so's Dad could talk me out of the unpopular decision.

Aunt Rita wouldn't allow me to call her aunt, and I lasted less than a month. A week after I got there she suggested I should think of finding another place to live. Rita is pretty, tiny and helpless looking. With tears in her innocent eyes she explained, "Jon, between the two of us, your parents don't know that I have a guy, and he sometimes stays overnight. Your being here complicates things."

I told her how I was not a child and tried to laugh it off. "After all, Aunt Rita, I watch *Dynasty*."

She went right on to tell me that her guy was married and didn't like other people *watching him*. I never did get to know his name. Aunt Rita introduced him to me as "my guy." He was grouchy, not at all like a TV cheat. I moved, but kept receiving my mail at Aunt Rita's. Sneaky, okay? But necessary for my parents' peace of mind.

Finding a decent place to live in New York City is grim business. Even skid-row flop houses have waiting lists. The homeless stake out special spaces in railroad- and bus-terminal waiting rooms. Like other foolish optimists, I was searching for a private place of my own. Real estate people look you dead in the eye and say $800, $900, over $1,000 and even much, much more. That's for a month, not a year. Hey, who wants to owe somebody $1,000 every thirty days? I'd have to be rich or else work at something illegal, maybe both. Rental agents smiled with a sneer while explaining their fee and the landlord's advance security payment. I followed up some newspaper ads, space to *share*. After viewing six health hazards and meeting three psychos, I happened on Harper Mead's place. It was one flight up, a back apartment, with a narrow glimpse of the Hudson River, use of the kitchen, bath and living area, and my very own private room. Not a loft or an L-shaped corridor section, but a for-real room with bookshelves, a desk, a bed, and at a decent price. But for all that, Harp himself was the reason I shook hands on the deal. He made me feel welcome. I had Perrier on the rocks. He downed white wine. I don't like alcohol or soda, but I hated to seem too young and square. I wanted apple juice, but Perrier has a more sophisticated, worldly sound. Harper said, "Good for you, one lush in a household is enough." He sure made me feel like there was nothing to worry about.

He's taller than I am, but that's not hard to be. I'm five feet nine inches. I guess he's six feet or better. A feeling came over me like we had met before—and all of it was happening again. Before he smoothed back his hair I knew he was going to do it. I also knew he'd draw his chair an inch closer. Hey, he could be an older age in the life of my first friend, Jimmy. They didn't look alike except for the dark reddish hair and that unhurried walk. But he sure reminded me of Jim.

Harp's living room is set up for *living*, neat but kinda crowded. Motion-picture stuff, projectors, cameras, books, magazines and more books. One whole wall is covered with film posters. In a corner there's a personal computer that makes my portable look almost like gametime under little Junior's Christmas tree. He explained the hodgepodge of equipment. "Jonathan, two years ago I decided to go entrepreneur. Work for myself and pay myself. I've done it. I'm a lecturer, demonstrator, general consultant, whatever is up for grabs. A producer of all and sundry. I'm now into documentary film. It's usually a feast or a famine here. I can manage everything you see, except that new personal computer."

"Well, Harper," I said, trying to sound older than seventeen.

"Harp is better."

"Okay, Harp, I can show you the ropes on your PC. I'm ready and able to pay my way for a good while, but I am presently unemployed, looking for a job."

"Enough said. You're on board. Maybe we'll get to share a few jobs as well as the apartment. Harper Mead is *never* unemployed, okay?"

He's a very direct person. I liked that. His mind is a fast fencer. Mine is a slow chess player. I worked with him on a couple of projects. We were a good team. Harp introduced me to the best days of my life. I was happy. One Saturday, six weeks after I moved in, we soundproofed my room with cork tiles and carpet to make it into a homemade recording and screening studio. I moved into his room.

But on the down side, it's kinda hard to let anybody take over your whole life, even if it's someone you love and admire most of the time.

That same person, the one closest to me, Harper Mead, became the super rat of my life. "Not to worry." He likes to say that, while worrying the hell out of you. He said it just before my first "coming out" meeting, which was a half-dozen of us in a tiny room, sharing a jug of wine. After a lot of talk about gay courage and commitment, we got down to the business at hand. One guy started it off. "My name is Ronnie, and I'm gay." Damn, I found it hard not to laugh. Others went through the same routine, ripping off a page from Alcoholics Anonymous. Harp took the next turn and made his declaration straight out, with tough gung-ho pride. I almost wanted to step forward and pin a medal on his chest.

Then I tried to do what they had done. "My name is Jonathan Barnett . . ." I sure the hell couldn't. I did explain, "I don't want to say it here when I know I wouldn't say it on the outside. You all may know what I am and others might take a guess, but it's a drag to come out, no pun intended. Hell, it's my closet, I can live in it if I want to."

Harp tried to shame me into going along with the program. He thinks a few years' seniority gives him the right to guide my thinking. "Jon, that stuff is pure chicken. What you want is to have it both ways. You want to live a bent life while passing for straight."

One really older guy was there. At home Harp had laughingly warned me, "You'll meet a pitifully over-fifty swish Nellie." Well, that Nellie spoke up and defended me in a defiant, high, trembly voice. I laughed along when Harp had called him a swish Nellie, but an alarm sounded in my gut. Why make fun of the swishy guy? His honesty became our joke, right? Well, that Nellie was the only one who spoke up for me. "Jon, it takes time to find out who you are. And then you need even more time to accept that. So, dear boy, you just do or don't do your do. But if and when you do—please do and say it the way you damned well want it done."

I welcomed his support, but had to make a correction. "Well, I think I know what I am. But I don't care to make public announcements about it. Show me a straight who says 'My name is John Doe and I'm a heterosexual.' Declaring myself to others, that's not for me. I don't like it." There was a small chorus of shoutdowns and more encouragement from the Nellie. Support sure can come from unexpected places.

After the meeting Harp was mad. He said I had publicly denied our relationship. He really lashed out against me about it. At home, after killing a bottle of red wine, he sent me to the store for aspirin and then made that phone call. My mother is now two steps away from cracking up, that's what Harp's done for her. However, face it, if I wasn't exactly who and what he says I am, he would not have had anything to tell.

I left Marsley Falls for New York City in the first place to save my parents from handling what they didn't want to see or talk about. Well, Harp blew that. So I had to go back home to explain. But they wouldn't let me.

My father dropped some good thoughts in my head as I was growing up. One was that a certain part of us belongs to ourselves. He answered my questions most of the time, but once in a while he'd say, "I prefer to keep that item to myself for the moment." Often, while filling out income tax forms and other papers, he'd shake his black and gray mane of hair and complain: "Computers know my age, income, birthplace, the cost of the house, how much dental work is in my mouth and on and on ad infinitum. Every day I have to search harder to find a scrap of myself that remains unknown to a million prying machines. A bit of truth, left undisturbed in some secret corner of my thought, that is mine and mine alone." He's right about that.

When I left Harp and went back home to Marsley Falls to say hello and so long to my parents, my very first stop was Fern's house. My girlfriend. Fern Clark never seems to expect too much of anybody. Her favorite song is "I Love You Just the Way You Are." She has a delicate air. Looks like maybe she's coming from another time and place. Way out in the future or far back in the past, but not quite here. Well, offbeat.

Fern, Jim and I, the three of us, we shared early childhood from kindergarten through high school. We quietly worked for hours doing homework together.

Some years ago Fern's dad bought her a computer. That was kinda his livelihood, selling software to business outfits. Mr. Clark taught us a lot. Fern's house became a second home to me and my buddy Jimmy. We liked being there. One day Mom asked me to take Fern to a high school freshman party. Somebody on faculty had the sudden idea of boys escorting girls to a "Frosh Fest." Soon there were only a few girls left waiting to be asked. One of them was Fern. How could that be? Every guy would want to escort her. She was better than just plain pretty, and still is. She's only beautiful. Amber eyes, like, turned on by some sweet mystery. While growing up we were always together. Movies, swimming, skating, playing games and stuff, but that was not dating; that's just living.

My mother pushed me into our first date after Fern's dad hinted that she was turning down other guys because she was waiting for one certain particular person, *me.* I was glad to take her. I hadn't asked anybody because I hadn't planned on going. Since Jimmy didn't have a date either, we both took Fern. The three of us were always a combo anyway. A gang of guys asked her to dance. She seemed to avoid most of them, except me, kind of shy, sort of—that's her way.

Fern's always attractive but doesn't go in too much for makeup and mushing over guys. She lost her mother at age nine. Her father looked after her alone, except for a daily housekeeper, a nice colored lady named Miss Dorothy. Miss Dorothy knows how to make good things from apples, which we picked off their backyard tree.

Going home, my very first stop had to be at Fern's, for coffee, conversation and an apple turnover. I told her I was into a bad time, how postponing college for a year wasn't working. I couldn't tell her much else except that I was down for the count and needing time out between rounds. She came up with a solution.

"Why not take the temporary job I'm about to turn down? It's fifty miles north, teaching personal computer at Minitown High. Jon, when they say Mini, believe it. A smaller town than our Marsley Falls. A sleepy-looking place. It's square country. The school has a small bank of new computers, but the bottom line is *low* pay. However, if you're going through a tough time, why not work and collect a little cash to ease your current pain?"

"Hmm, Minitown. Seems I've heard of it. Anyplace to live?"

She told me about this studio apartment in a private home near school, within walking distance, and the rent was low. "Hey, Fern," I said, "where's the catch? Why don't you want the job?"

"Well," she said, "it was a temptation, but I decided

to stick with two-year prep now, business major. If I drop out like you I might never get back. I don't have your smarts. However, if I was not leaving town, I'd sure try to keep you here near me. I think about you a lot."

"And I think about you, Fern."

"Talk on, Jon."

"Like I said, I'm going through tough stuff. Oh, damn it, I'd like to tell you something about myself, but it might make you think less of me."

"Then don't tell it. Please, I don't want to hear it. Later on you may be sorry you said it and spoil . . . our later relationship. No negatives! Anyway, you're smart enough to solve whatever it is. When we were kids, remember the birthday that Jimmy gave me a giant jigsaw puzzle? Each silly birch tree looked like the next. A maze of brown and white. But you solved it fast."

"Fern, that was easy. I thought of shapes. I didn't look for colors and trees. I turned that puzzle on the wrong side and matched it up without studying the confusion."

"Jon, do that with your present problem. When you solve it, please tell me. I've missed you so."

"Same here."

"Thanks for the great letters. We still belong to the mutual admiration society, right?"

"Yeah, we're two true-blue members."

"Jimmy's no longer number three?"

"Oh, England's too far away for him to qualify."

"Good. I'm glad there's just the two of us. Jon, when you get to Minitown—"

"I don't have the job yet, Fern."

"Oh, you'll get it if you want it. The course is an elective—small temporary group. If they'd take me, they'll love getting you. See you tonight at dinner. Oh, your mother didn't tell you I'm invited?"

"Well now I bet that's her surprise. She promised a surprise."

"Jon, did you happen to leave a special girl back in New York?"

"No, I did not. But there's something else I want to tell about."

"Never mind anything else. Look, Jon, if you ever have an important, first-rate question to ask a girl, try it out on me first, okay?"

"You bet. Sure."

"And solve your dumb problem damn soon. Just turn it on the wrong side and look at it that way so you won't get confused."

Before I left home again, my parents talked about everything under the sun except *gay* stuff. I tried to bring it up. Mom kept turning me off. "Jon, let that nonsense rest for a bit."

Dad sang the same song. "Son, look at it this way, life goes on and keeps changing every day. Don't worry about old autumn leaves. Soon a brisk wind will come along and sweep things clean."

One of my grade school teachers once asked my parents, "Aren't you folks proud of his grades?" Dad rumpled my hair and said, "He's a good kid and that's all that really counts."

Grad classmates teased me about making high averages. "Batting a thousand as usual?" No sweat. I liked turning problems around until answers popped up. Studying a textbook was never my problem. I sent in four college applications and three put out the welcome mat. It was really hard for my folks to accept a year-ahead, top-of-the-class kid dropping out, even temporarily. Everyday living, now there's a private subject I always seem to flunk. I fail on—picking who to like, who to love, even who and what to believe in. I'm a pick-it-wrong guy. Maybe that's why I keep running. Too chicken, like Harp says. Too cowardly to stand my ground and face the future.

2 Jonathan Barnett

I THOUGHT A BUS COULD CARRY ME AWAY FROM hassles. So next I was on the way to this place, Minitown. On the bus I ran into the beginning of another screwup. It was hot. A September scorcher. The air conditioner was only half working. A girl got on just a few stops before Minitown and climbed all over me to sit by the window. That's what I get for liking aisle seats.

She moved around a lot. I leaned away to give the restless one more room. She sat down, took a lacy handkerchief from her purse and fanned her neck. Wow! Perfume hit the air. A double dose of violets. No, it was lilac. My mother grows a lilac bush by the side of our house. The gal kept squirming. Maybe she had eaten a can of worms for lunch.

"Sorry," I said, "am I crowding?"

She snapped, "No, it's just that hot weather sucks." A pretty girl, pretty crude.

"Forget it, *Miss*. I just asked."

"No sweat, *Mister*. Where you going?"

"To Minitown, as a stranger."

"Good. You can sit in Mini Park, watch us natives go by and laugh yourself to death."

"I've heard it's an up-and-going town."

"Right. Everybody gets up and goes because nothing's going on. If I were you I'd head for another place."

"So why don't you do that?"

"I was born there. Live there. Under age, I'm trapped."

Shielded by sunglasses I studied her rounded face. Too young to come on so bitter. She was also nosy.

"Do you have a girlfriend?"

"Yes."

"What's her name and where does she live?"

"Fern lives in Marsley Falls."

"What are you going to do in my town? Or is it a secret?"

"Teach."

"Got it. You're the new teenage computer instructor for Minitown High."

"How did you know?"

"News leaks out of the principal's office. Well, maybe I'll break down, throw up and take your crumby computer course. Of course, nobody has to take it really."

"Gee, thanks. I'll send that out as a press release. 'Student broke down, threw up and took the crumby . . .' "

"Oh, you're a fresh ass. I love it. Sassy. Mini High needs another one besides me. I'm Theodora Lynn. Just been to the next town to secretly see my head shrinker."

"I'm Jonathan Barnett."

"And you don't like to talk much."

"No, I don't."

She opened a book. Tapered fingers beautifully manicured. From the corner of my eye I saw longish blond hair to her shoulders. Fern Clark has shiny brown hair with lots of sparkly gold highlights in it. Fern is plainly pretty, neat.

Buses travel through some bottom-of-the-barrel territory. We made one pickup stop across from a shabby bar and grill. A few thin-faced, hungry-looking guys hung out in front, laughing about nothing in particular. The scene was downright funky looking. Inside of that bar the ambience must have been dim, grimy and damp. I recalled thinking how if I felt like a complete failure I might have been hanging out there with them, drunk and trying to act *manly*. If I was a drug addict I'd have been stoned, out of it, refusing to see myself or deal with reality. However, not being into numbing my head, there I was riding along sober and hurting, staring deep into my private blues. However, that's not a chicken kind of high—soberly looking straight at your low moment, facing harsh reality with the naked eye. But I still halfway envy those guys. It might be a gas just to stand in front of a scroungy dive, acting macho, sipping at a can of beer wrapped in a brown paper bag. Maybe it feels free to be looking mean, like you're not to be hassled. One long, tall black guy was out there spitting and wiping one corner of a generous mouth on his ragged, dirty, plaid shirt-sleeve. After the stream of tobacco saliva had hit the curbstone, he threw the bus a mean look, like he might just run over and attack us all. There are days when I feel spittin' mean, just like that. Sometimes you need to feel threatening 'cause you're fed up with being patient and understanding with a world full of uppity jerks. Particularly one like that Harper Mead who doesn't know shit from Tofutti. I stretched out, pretending to nap. I was sleepily glad to get away from home, looking forward to seeing something new.

The girl sitting next to me on that Minitown bus, Theodora Lynn, started gabbing about nothing—complaining about the weather. If it wasn't for weather, what would pushy strangers talk about? Shit, unless you're a farmer, who the hell cares if it's as cold today as it was yesterday? Who cares if it's warmer than this morning? Who cares if it might rain? I adjusted my blackout sun shades to let her know I'd had enough.

Dark glasses shut out and drive people up the wall. They keep out intruders. Back in New York City folks obey shutout signals—as easy as reading red and green traffic lights. Of course, they don't pay traffic signals too much exact mind. They hop around cars and go skittering in between fenders, sort of fancy street dancing. Once in a while one drifts into an offbeat rhythm and his butt goes sailing through the air. Comes a blast of car horns, then ambulances, police sirens and, once in a while, a quick, sad, final exit.

There I was drowsing along, riding my bus, visualizing Harp. Imagining him doing a dumb jaywalk on a Broadway crossing. Suddenly he went off his rhythm, missed a hot-dog wagon, ran into a blue ten-speed bike, flew over the hood of a yellow cab, and his arrogant, stubborn behind flew high and slammed down hard on a big jagged slab of broken sidewalk. Concrete flew! Blood gushed and splattered red, red, red. A beautiful little infant girl was thrown from her baby carriage. She landed safely in my waiting, outstretched arms. In the 1,000th part of a split second, I returned the still sleeping, smiling child to her weeping but grateful mother. The crowd applauded me. Curious bystanders surrounded Harp's torn, bleeding, quivering carcass. They had the medics locked out. I held up one strong, determined hand and the crowd parted. I spoke down to him, not even pointing an accusing finger, and said, "I'll forgive you, Harp, but you are dying like a dog for the dirty deed you did."

A four-star fantasy. I only wish I could truly wish him dead. The truth is he was the best thing that ever happened to me in so many ways. I hate myself for missing those better times.

The young bus lady on my left broke through the reverie. She said, "Remember, my name is Theodora Lynn. I am the very first student you met. It's fate, wouldn't you say?"

I held her off by faking a soft snore. Strange people always want to talk to me. She had the nerve to reach over and lift the sunglasses off my face. Nose to nose she stared in my eyes. I rescued the shades. She said, "You are terribly young to be, like, an instructor."

"Theo, I'm fast growing older by the minute."

"Jonathan, guess what? You're replacing our phys ed teacher at Mini High. Believe you me, I don't think he likes the idea."

"How come?"

"He has to audit your course. Has to learn from a teenager so he can take over your class and *replace you* next year. I hate dirty tricks, okay?"

"Oh, no sweat, I'll be in college next year—but thanks for telling. You feel like a real kindred spirit."

"What the hell is that?"

"It means two people who are related because they have a lot in common."

Tears welled in her eyes. One spilled over and ran down her cheek. She said, "Wow, that's fantastic. I'm a Pisces. What's your sign?"

"Libra."

Theo turned radiant. Dried her cheek with the lilac-scented handkerchief and gracefully extended her hand. She has a lovely smile.

A bus ride not too long ago. Now Theodora's questionable honor, and mine, is up for grabs. So is the teacher's, a teacher named Rex Hardy. I wish I could trust some one person enough to tell exactly what I'm feeling. A person who wouldn't laugh or give out too much "If I were you" talk. When people say that, they really mean, "If I were you I'd be *me*." According to everyone I know they all could expertly run my life better than I can. But I'm the one who has to wake up each morning and solve the puzzle of the day all by myself—on my own. My mind is the only one I have for full-time use.

Lataweeze, my cat, is sleepy but still watching. Animals are proud, independent and also dependent at the same time. That's not easy.

3 Tyrone Tate

JONATHAN BARNETT IS MY COMPUTER INSTRUC-tor. He's not my "too-close guy" like some crumb-ass anonymous phone caller says he is. But he's not my enemy, I don't think. I'm not his, okay? That's it. We're not truly in trouble, but being witnesses to an attempted sex attack is serious stuff. I could get summoned to court. Strangers trying to burn down our house is also serious. Very.

Mini High is almost all right. It could be okay if it wasn't for gritty happenings. At least they have some computers here. There wasn't even one in my last school. I telephoned how everything is going, to my old friend Dudley. He lives back in Bedford Stuyvesant, Brooklyn, which is like Harlem. I miss having friends. I used to live in Crown Heights, which is the next bus or subway stop out of Bed Stuy. They're both black neighborhoods, but whites are no way new to me. They used to come to our house to read the gas meter. They ran supermarkets, and an awful lot of them are policemen.

Whites did street repairs, digging down to the broken pipes. They fixed traffic lights, dug up sidewalks. Boarded up empty buildings and all like that. I saw plenty of them. But they were just doing jobs. You don't really know who they are—working. Working they seem to slide right on past your eyesight. Every evening they quit and go off to somewhere else. This Minitown might be one of the places where some of them went.

Did you ever get stuck under an ice-cold shower and not a drop of warm water mixed in? Can you imagine diving in the Atlantic Ocean on a cold day in January? Did you ever have a weird dream with a lot of strange sci-fi silent people staring at you? They're, like, in a circle and you're in the middle, buck naked. Nothing to protect yourself and no place to hide. Well, being black in an all white school, with all white teachers, feels kind of like that. Some look at me like I'm from outer space. My sister Susan is fifteen and I'm fourteen. We're the only blacks.

White teachers and students come in two kinds of packages, chilly or over-friendly. The friendly ones look like they feel sorry for me. I look back like I'm sorry for them. You learn to defend yourself. All was not A-OK back in Bed Stuy and Crown Heights. But there were not too many sudden surprises either. I knew every public school exit in case some tough wanted to beat me up just to prove that he could. That's how come I did so well at track. I learned how to take off and make time. I had to pass crack pushers on both sides of my school street. Man, the TV and radio are telling you to say no.

But they don't say how best to do it. My friend Dudley told me. "Tyrone, if you wake up in a cage and find your hand in a hungry lion's mouth, make no sudden moves. Go slow and *ease* your hand free. Always say no in a smooth way, like, 'Thanks, my man, but I'm in trainin' and have to take a piss test in the mornin'.'" Now, nobody's giving any urine exam, but saying so might back a pusher kinda off. Could be he wouldn't even talk to you much anymore. The idea of a kid being tested might make some hustlers not want to deal around that kind of school. Dudley's smart. He's always lived in Bed Stuy and knows the score. Knows even more than those of us who live in Crown Heights. I do try to remember to ease my hand out of any lion's mouth. Particularly these slick, human ones who prowl Minitown. Nice neighborhoods do ugly things just like bad neighborhoods. But it's harder to catch them at it.

In Crown Heights, for a while my folks put me and Susan in private school—Greystone, grades eight through twelve. It was expensive, neat and *boring*. About one-fourth BLACK students and two BLACK teachers out of twelve. We might have stayed on there but my father made too much money for us to get any scholarships. Dad sells Moderna-Trend beauty products franchises. He sells people permission to sell the product, then they order all of it through him. He still keeps his office in Brooklyn. Mom used to put in part-time teaching at Greystone. Music appreciation. That helped pay our tuitions. She was working herself to death on account of two tuitions, and helping Dad with franchise paperwork and stuff. Moderna-Trend is mostly about the hair relaxing business. Mom's hair is relaxed so fine that in a slight breeze it will float. My sister, Susan, stays into natural hair. Bushed or braided, but never relaxed. She says, "I'm not going to straighten my hair or nose in order to fit into anybody's mainstream." She bugs Dad with that remark.

My parents figured that moving out of town would allow them to invest our tuition money into a house. They also thought a suburban public school would be as good as big-city private. Dad sold the old house for big bucks, then added our tuition money to buy this fine home. So here we are.

Susie says she catches it harder 'cause she's the only girl of her race. Me, I can deal with any bad vibes at school. I'm into that. But, in this town, home is another matter. In Crown Heights you never had to watch for rough stuff in both places—school *and* next door to where you live. We sure moved into one neat-looking hornets' nest. Another middle-class B-L-A-C-K family lived over in the next county, but they're now moving to someplace farther out yet. And they're happier than ever. Dad says they enjoy being the only ones.

My father's now got me programmed so I'm spelling B-L-A-C-K under my breath, with my head down and my mouth twisted to one side like prisoners talk on old late-night TV movies. Maybe we're not cut out to be the *only* ones. Some BLACK people can move into an all W-H-I-T-E situation with no sweat. Everything about them turns, like, W-H-I-T-E except their color. Some are now even working on that. Yeah, they're makin' it into the solid mainstream. I think Dad is gettin' there. He jumped on Susan for sayin' "I'm proud of my black heritage." He squared back his six-foot frame and came on, like, ready to blow a fuse, but he whispered. In this ranch-style, four-bedroom, brick-faced, central-air-conditioned house with a swim pool and two-car garage, all arguments are *whispered,* and touchy words are quietly spelled out. After all, can't have W-H-I-T-E-S tuned in on B-L-A-C-K disagreement.

Maxwell Tate, my father, must think W-H-I-T-E folks can't spell. He's always spelling out B-L-A-C-K and W-H-I-T-E. Mom's almost as bad as he is these days. She's also into whispers. Shaking her relaxed hair and saying, "We have to make this thing work. It's life and death. We're at the point of no return. Too deep in to turn back. Debts up to our back teeth! If we don't love it here we can't leave it. So please everybody just love it, love it, love it. This has to work." She's even sayin' that when there's no reason. Cutting up bananas over cereal, "This thing has to work."

I got to get in a ha-ha somewhere. So I asked, "What has to work, the banana?"

She said, "You know exactly what I mean, Tyrone. We have to stay here and get along, no matter that we are the only ones. Hang on and make it. Blend in, fit in and speak decent English. You deliberately leave *ings* off your word endings."

"Ma, so do white kids."

"Everybody will jump on you harder, that's the nature of racism."

"Ma, Dad says that race doesn't matter."

"Tyrone, shut up, behave and stop calling me Ma. Say Mother, Mommy or Mom. And stop calling Susan, Susie."

"Can I still call grandma, Gaga?"

"No, damn it. Show a little class." She looked, like, ready to cry.

Dad came hurrying into the kitchen with a whispered warning. "Cut out the loudness. I bet people can hear our B-L-A-C-K business all the way to the train station. Keep your voices *down*."

Susan glided in from the back patio, looking powerful in her fine new Egyptian caftan, her hair in tiny long braids swinging around—five hundred of them she claims. It cost $110 to have it done at the Brooklyn Black Braidery. It takes an awful lot of money to be natural. She said, "Dad, I for one am definitely proud of my black heritage—and my African ancestry." He quietly gave her hell.

"Susan, everybody in town can see what we are. Why do you have to announce forty times a day that you are B-L-A-C-K. In the first place you and Tyrone are the only dark spots at Mini High. You can definitely be seen, so don't try to gild the lily by going on about heritage. And don't forget we're living next door to a racist. The Lynns probably think each and every male—W-H-I-T-E and B-L-A-C-K—is after their daughter Theodora. And her daddy is no Archie Bunker. The real thing is never funny."

Susan went into her latest theme song. "I'm now at dating age. I'm the *only* black girl in a white school. And there's no boy of my own kind to be with. If I go out with a white one, everybody will say I'm loose. Who's my escort ever to be?"

Dad gave one of his sighs and took care of it in a sentence. "When an escort is needed, go with your brother."

Sis flipped. "That looks like incest. I'll just keep writing and calling my guy back in Crown Heights. We'll date by mail and phone. Safe sex, right?"

Dad lifted his voice above a whisper. "Damn it, fifteen is too young to have a guy or sex. I moved this family an hour and a half away from a drug-dealing block to give you a better life."

Mom played peacemaker. "Susan, we will go back to visit Brooklyn sometime."

Me, I suggested we invite all of Brooklyn to come here and visit. "Susan's right, Dad. Being an only is weird. Every trouble that pops up, all eyes are on us."

Since my father's pulling down maybe $70,000 a year, he's getting awfully edgy. Complains how he has to *spend* $80,000 to make $50,000 out of the seventy thou. Weird mathematics. Now he's planning to take out bank loans for us to go to good colleges. Making that much money, seems like we wouldn't have to borrow. He says mainstream economics is about credit, not cash.

Another thing, he doesn't too often ask his own brother, Uncle Kwame, out here to Minitown. Last week he told me, "Let Kwame keep his rabble-rousing black self at home. Every time there's a new street demonstration in the city he's on the evening news in the front line carrying some kind of message on a stick. 'Free this one and free that one.' When a cop cracked Kwame's head and dragged his backside off to jail, who did he use his one phone call on? Me, that's who. And I put up that bail. He shows no respect. Makes fun of every upward move I make. Doesn't mind holding a hand out for my money. But he won't do what I do to earn enough to have some. Always willing to let me take the commercial lumps. People don't care where money comes from if you give or lend it to them. They grab it with trembling hands and look for more, while criticizing you. Tell me, why in hell does he call himself Kwame? What's wrong with his real name, Fred? Also I happen to know 'Kwame' is an African name that means *born on Saturday*. He was born on a Monday!"

Susan gave him a hug and a serious look. "Dad, Uncle Kwame is proud of his African heritage and he's claiming it the best way he knows. Please don't stop loving him, and don't let this Minitown—and other people and their ways—stop us from loving each other." She cried and swung her pretty braids sadly.

Dad held an arm out to me and another to Mom and Susan. "Okay, we're going to love each other no matter what, right Arlene?"

Mom smiled. "That's right, Max. No matter what." But they were looking worried.

My mother's pretty enough, but this year she dieted herself down from a size thirteen to a seven. Mom says upwardly mobile women must be thin. She stays kinda trembly hungry. No joke, being upper middle class is hard work. She begged Dad not to credit card more debt just to buy her a new fur coat. He said, "Now we're in mainstream America, so take a dive and swim, baby, swim. I want you to wear a full-length mink. We'll buy it on discount so you can walk down our driveway and send that next-door cracker stone out of his feeble mind. Somebody's trying to burn down our house? Okay, let them. If we survive we'll collect insurance and move to a classier address. This jive-time neighborhood is not top quality nohow. Anyway our neighbor, Mr. Lynn, is going to need a straitjacket when he finds out they accepted me in the country club. I hear he's been turned down twice. Ha! He who laughs last, laughs best. Susan, by the way, comb out those braids sometime. And at least let your head *look* relaxed. I can't sell relaxer and have a family member going in the opposite direction."

I know Susie, she's going to braid or unbraid whenever she pleases. She's stubborn.

However, Dad was glad we both took Compu-One, Barnett's class, even though it's not compulsory. If we hadn't he'd have had a fit. My father expects us to get top marks in everything, or else. First thing he suggested was "Don't tell the instructor that you have your own computer at home."

"Why not?" I asked.

"Tyrone, if he thinks you're starting off without one it will make you look smarter. Boy, learn the tricks of the trade."

"What trade?"

"The business of getting on in their world."

"I thought you said race doesn't matter."

"Did I mention race?"

"No, but you called it *their* world."

He looked down for a second. Then came back stronger. "So life is a little confusing. Race should not matter. But, damn it, every day somebody sees that it does. However tough the road, we are Americans, born in America, and we're going to forge straight ahead, looking for life and liberty while pursuing the happiness part."

He has come a long way. From the bottom on up to Minitown. But when we left Crown Heights to move here, Uncle Kwame called Dad an Oreo cookie. That is a real put-down name. Someone who's black on the outside and white on the inside—no longer interested in the fate of their own people. They stopped speaking for a month. Gaga, my grandmother, called them long distance from Georgia and made them make up.

I'm crazy about Uncle Kwame. But I wish he wouldn't call my dad Uncle Tom names. My father's mainly afraid our new white neighbors will find out that his brother gets on TV and in jail for protesting. However they're all now on *my* case, including Mom and Susan. They won't exactly say it, but they're into trying to make me lie in order to stay out of W-H-I-T-E trouble. If the Lynns go to court about their daughter, Theodora, I might be summoned to testify under oath. I'll have to say I saw the phys ed teacher, Mr. Hardy, in the hall closet with her, and her clothing was torn. That's the truth. I did see them. Jonathan Barnett and I, we both saw them. Dad and Uncle Kwame are united against me saying what I saw. I *know* what I saw. They've abandoned talk about justice and truth because Hardy, and Spencer Reese, a student, and other people, WHITE people, are spreading word that Barnett is gay. My family doesn't want me to look like I'm too close to him. Bet they're scared other people might think I'm also gay. The next thing they might think is that if you're gay you could have Acquired Immune Deficiency—AIDS. So now it's dangerous to say what I saw, because people might think all that. Damn, Barnett is my instructor, can I pretend not to know him? Uncle Kwame warned me stay away from the "controversial" instructor. Dad keeps saying, "When Theo and that Rex Hardy were caught together, you were looking the other way and didn't see anything. Ty, keep your nose and reputation clean. After all, you don't see too well anyway. You need glasses, got it?" Now what kind of talk is that? Back in Crown Heights we all used to think better. Minitown's crackin' us up. If this house gets burned down altogether instead of just up one side of the building, maybe we'll get to move and go back to our own people. But I hope we don't really get burned out or we might all end up dead and not have to worry about which neighborhood to live in, right?

4 *Jonathan Barnett*

IT WAS GREAT TO GET INTO THIS APARTMENT. All mine. Moving in was one hang-free feeling. The cat, Lataweeze, was waiting on the doorstep. She took to me right off. Followed me in. The landlady, Mrs. Trale, disapproved. "Don't let her enter. She's nothing but a common stray. I fed that cat once in a while. But if you're too good to her she'll just hang around."

"Well, wouldn't anybody, Mrs. Trale?"

"She's also a *female.* Next thing you know there'll be kittens unless she's already altered."

I knew I was going to keep the cat no matter what the landlady said. So I tried to distract her with flattery. "You sure keep a nice-looking house, Mrs. Trale."

She wouldn't shake loose from studying the cat with a pitying look. "She's some kind of alley mixture. If I was going to take in a feline, which I'm not, I'd go to a breeder and buy one with background papers. I don't like a nobody, human or animal."

Next I admired her fake fireplace. She bit on that and

proudly explained the gas logs. "It gives enough warmth to knock the chill off until time for heavy heat. But don't forget to light the gas. A leak can be dangerous. Well, Mr. Barnett—enjoy your studio."

It was Saturday. No school. A brisk, windy, early fall rain was beating at the window. I stretched out on the single bed, staring up at a ceiling decorated with old-fashioned plaster curlicue designs. A border of grapes and leaves.

The "studio" is a room on the smallish side, but all mine. My own private bathroom for the first time in my life. Mrs. Trale wasn't too bad. In fact she used to be kinda pleasant until lately. Privacy is great, but nothing is one hundred percent. Nobody to talk to about present troubles. Can't call home. Can't call Harp, certainly not. Best not to ring Fern either. Getting too close might give her a wrong signal.

That first day here was good. Raindrops against the window—reminded me how I pitched pebbles to call Jim. We used to signal that way, throwing a few pebbles against windows.

This room is furnished with a large leather armchair and a patched hassock. A small table serves as the reading and eating place. There's a desk and bookshelves. In the cabinet drawers are a few knives, forks, spoons, a can opener and a thing to turn pancakes. In the oven I found two dented pots, a frying pan and a colander with one handle. It was like a secondhand treasure hunt. Made me remember going out with Harp, looking up good freebee junk on Thursday mornings. After five in the afternoon we'd celebrate with wine spritzers and pizza. He drank the wine. I drank only the spritz part, the seltzer.

Here and now, in the gloomy present, my radio is tuned to cool jazz. Wow! What a surprise from the local station. The imitation Tiffany table lamp throws a cozy ruddy glow around the room. But privacy hurts when you're in trouble. Lataweeze paws at her nose, takes a slow walking turn and settles on her pillow for a snooze. Faithful girl. The phone rings and rings. I don't answer. Anonymous calls scare me.

Taking my life is a lousy serious idea. Especially since I haven't really lived long enough to make an exit. I sure wish I had someone to talk to. Someone who wouldn't try to ridicule me because of what I feel. Someone to just listen. I don't need anybody who gives out nothing but pity. Pity is crumby comfort. I think of suicide, but I know I won't do it. Just a thought, that's all. I can picture everybody crying like crazy and feeling damn sorry that they didn't understand me.

Lately I've read a lot of books on gays. Some written by gays. Coming out sounds easy if you listen to those like Harp. But what if it hurts other people? Okay, a deep thought. We have twelve years of childhood, then only seven short ones to get past our teen years. Thirteen through nineteen, right? After that the adult trip is longer and leads into old age. Hmm . . . with a little luck, that is. I've almost served out my teen time. Maybe I won't make it much further. But I'd like to hang around for a while. I dig life. I go for sunsets, music, hiking, people-watching, new movies, old movies, sci-fi, hi-fi and just being. And I'm young enough to get in on that big bash of a New Year's Eve party, the last night of 1999, when all the living will walk straight into the year 2000. It will be ten hundred more years before anybody gets a chance to celebrate another thousandth anniversary. In 2000 I'll be twenty-nine. Not really old. That's gonna be one rocking New Year's Eve, if the big chiefs of the world don't blow away the planet before we get to really explore and improve it. And also if the streets are more dangerous than they are now. Cops could be shouting over bullhorns—"Stay in your homes! Come out at your own risk!" Hey, who wants to make that? If I should die before I wake—that old childhood prayer skips through my head. But why should I die before I wake? Screw suicide. Dying while you are awake is even harder.

So now I'm into thinking of my friend Jim, way overseas in England. I bet he'd *sincerely* feel sorry if I died. We became teenagers at the same time. Turned thirteen together. He was gawky and reddish with splotchy freckles all over his crooked face. He was a head taller then, probably still is, lucky dog. His mother had divorced his dad. He shared mine. Our house was, like, also his home, including our summer shack on Turnabout Mountain. Mom named it that because of the weird dirt road that led to our property. You drive uphill straight northward, then the road narrows, becomes steeper and returns south. You gotta get out and walk that last quarter mile, ending up almost where you started, except on a higher level. Dad bought the place for a rough-it retreat. He's no way a rough man. Dad's a high school history teacher, and his favorite exercise is *reading*—at home, on planes, at the seashore, in the mountains, anywhere, but mostly at home, where books line our living, dining and bedroom walls, and even the basement. *Roughing it* was something my father thought of for my sake.

During winter nights we spent hours planning our rough-it place. Dad bought how-to books and outlined big projects. "Well, son . . ." He'd start off like that when talking togetherness things. "Well, son, first we'll mend that leaky roof or put on a new one." Mom smiled happily on all of our schemes, even though she knew most of them would fall through. Another plan was to build a good fence across the road at the entrance. We were going to split our own rails, Dad announced, "Just like good old Abe Lincoln." On and on he'd go, buying blueprints and pictures of chicken coops and sheds or whatever else some expert had written up in a do-it-yourself book. But spring, summer and early fall caught us with little or nothing done because of using up most of his time on writing research papers, book reports and reviews, or going to lecture at out-of-town historical meetings. So, as rugged as it was, Turnabout became a place just to camp in our sleeping bags and cook outdoors now and then. I liked it. We never got to fix the roof or split any rails like Lincoln.

Jim's folks and mine let us hike up to Turnabout alone as long as we promised to take care and not go out during a storm. Once we almost fell through a dry-rotted place on the roof while trying to patch it. Another time Jim helpfully broke the handle off the kitchen water faucet and I cracked the sink trying to put it back on. We never reported the mishaps. No one worried about it. There was a workable pump in the backyard. The water tasted okay.

Oh, but that mountain air was clean and fresh, and we had a fine time sweating out days and freezing through nights. Good-bye, Turnabout. Wonder if I'll ever go up there again? If I do get back, Jim won't be there. Nothing stays the same. However, here I am in my very own apartment at last. Privacy's really great, but when there's trouble, who needs it?

5 Theodora Lynn

IT'LL SOON BE SHOW-DOWN TIME FOR THE school board and all others who don't care to know that Rex Hardy, a teacher, tried to rape me, a defenseless fifteen-year-old student. Good that Barnett's still on the scene. It helps to have one surefire honest witness, a true kindred soul. My dad claims Jonathan's too young to be an instructor. So what? For some mystic reason the two of us met on that hot bus. My horoscope for the day was "You are about to meet a fascinating stranger who will influence your life."

The next week I told my therapist about him. She said, "Theo, I'm glad to hear that at last there is one likeable male in your life." She was trying to hint that my problem is about who I like or don't like or that I'm desperately looking for a guy who will go for me. They always want to blame the poor victim. Barnett is not at all in any way my personal type for a boyfriend. He's simply a true kindred spirit. Someone who's like a part of myself. Both of us are naturally high-minded.

I remember how on the bus he practically begged me to take his course. How could I resist? After just a few classes I was way out front, running ahead of every smartass. Barnett was pleased. Some of the gals like Shelly, Barbara and Tony-Marie turned even more jealous than they already were. Eating their envious hearts out. All they know how to do is gab and gossip. It kills them that I'm into intellect and they are definitely not. Did I care that I wasn't invited to Tony-Marie's last party? No way. Big deal. She sent out printed invites. And served potato chips and apple juice! She made the social column in the *Minitown Press*. Some people in this town, every time they open a plastic cup of sour cream onion dip they call in a reporter to cover the event. Boring.

As for the male population of Mini High—a bunch of nerds. I walk down the corridor and guys are talking to me, trying to make a play. "You're what I want to get, Hotsy." Well I'm exactly what they haven't had and never will. I hate that "Hotsy." It's like saying I'm easy to score on. I didn't have to wait till I was fifteen to discover what a man wants. I have every male move figured out before they try to make it. A bunch of despicable one-track-mind sneaks.

Looking back—well maybe I should have just been born smarter. Guess I have dumb genes. Rex—Mr. Hardy, king of physical ed himself—loved to take me aside to discuss *my* problems. He's the one with problems. Always heavy breathing down my neck and talking crap about how I should show more interest in study. He showed so much interest in my anatomy that his head went to nutsville. The old lecher must be over forty and has ten very nervous flexible fingers. Rex is the master craftsman of the accidental bump. One day he deliberately stumbled into me, then, while picking up my books, he stole X-ray peeks through my blouse. The older the bolder, okay? Sexy Rexy, the guys call him. The girls, dumb as they are, all know how to duck his roaming hands while giggling like crass simpletons. I let him get away with a fast feel just one time. I had cribbed on remedial math. He was monitoring the test, just a monitor—and caught me copying off an answer written in the palm of my own hand, not from somebody else's paper. Being patted on the buns bugs me. But when caught skating on thin ice, what can you say? After class he blocked my way and whispered, "Watch it, honey," and then gave me a rub plus a pat. I took it. Stood still for about two seconds. Putting up with more might seem like a come-on, right? But I never "tempted and teased" him. I don't care what the liar tells other people. So one time he let me by on a slight cheat, okay? I took a pat on the buns just to say thanks. Wrong is wrong, but we were *both* wrong. Fifty-fifty wrong is not as wrong as if I was wrong all by myself.

Rex runs himself to death trying to impress Mrs. Mitchell, the principal. Mitch is a plain, no-nonsense widow woman with grown children. I bet she's ready to go to court and take an oath that Rex is the most trustworthy guy in town. A "gentleman," she likes to call him. So let him pat her butt, why doesn't she. However, credit where credit is due, even to a rapist. After getting town business people to raise the money, he bought Mini High ten personal computers at rock bottom discount. Problem is, he has to learn how to work one before he can teach it. Mitch called in Jonathan Barnett, young, good looking and smart. How's that for Hardy's competition? So Hardy has to *audit a kid's class*. Auditing is a way for Rex to *listen and learn*. Then he's going to snatch the instructor job for himself. Everybody knows he'll take over next year. Dirty tricks!

I was kind of proud to tell my dad when I joined the compu-class. After all, it's not compulsory. My father did not cheer. He slapped one hand down on the dining room table. "Don't you think it might help if you learned to read and write a little better before turning to machinery?" At our house we always go through the motions of theatrical democracy, putting on acts one and two before dropping the final curtain on another bad show. While taking stabs at peach cobbler, he gave up some stingy encouragement. "Your high school handwriting doesn't look as good as mine was in fourth grade. However, maybe a computer can save you the trouble of having to add, subtract or write anything for the rest of your life, so take it." He was upset because my second witness of the thing in the closet with Hardy had at that time just moved in next door. He's a member of the first black family in the neighborhood. Dad almost died the evening they came to check out the house. We were out back mending the fieldstone barbecue pit when our used-to-be neighbors, the blond, blue-eyed Foresters, brought home a very black man with a brown wife and two browner kids. The blacks got out of a shiny new Cadillac and boldly walked straight up the next-door walkway.

Danny Forester gloated. "Evening! Miss Lynn, Mr. and Mrs. Lynn. Meet Mr. and Mrs. Maxwell Tate, their son Tyrone and daughter Susan. Your new *neighbors*." Dad's face went beet red. That sneaky Danny. We never got along too well with him or his pouty skinny wife Anna. Once for a joke, I called her Anna Rexia. She didn't like it. No sense of humor. The blacks, the Tates, were dressed in their finest. Tate senior gave us a deep husky laugh. Just like he was on the same level as everyone else. "Good evening, neighbors-to-be." He acted so damn sure of himself. Awfully grand—considering.

They were not like Hank Thompson was. Hank taught a special course in school last year, modern tap dancing. I never once saw him when he wasn't smiling. Everyone liked him. He was so open and so—oh, nobody cared or even noticed how dark he was. He would do you a favor in a minute without your even asking. Why can't they all be that way? Purple, green or polka dot, nobody's against anybody when they're friendly like he was. But Hank went away. Just took off at the end of the year, unexpectedly. I don't know why he left.

Dad had some hot words for Danny Forester after the Tates looked over the property, shook hands and left, with Mr. Tate waving good-bye at us.

"What's going on, Forester?" Dad asked. "Is this a plot to downgrade my property? One last hate ploy before moving to California? Are you trying to make me look like a jackass in the real estate business?"

"Well, Lynn, you know the name of the game is—sell to the best buyer. Unlike you, I didn't sign any restrictive clause when I bought my place. When you sell yours, do it your way. You do your thing, I do mine, right?"

Big, broad Danny and long, lanky Dad. They marched and shouted, each on his side of the fence, until it looked like they were ready to jump the property line. Mrs. Forester and Mom stepped in to keep them from a hands-on demonstration. Dad came inside and right away phoned every neighbor on the block, warning them about the coming invasion. What really got him is that the Foresters' house is on the corner and ours is next to it. That makes us the only ones living next door to black people. Mom was concerned but she didn't panic.

I don't think my father is really prejudiced. He's not a *racist*, not like some of his friends. Dad likes watching TV stories about black and white policemen working as a team. He cheers when they catch a black criminal together. Mostly he applauds the black cop. "That's it. Now there's a great colored guy. He's not biased. Did you see how he saved his sidekick?" Dad likes them in sports too, watching those fast basketball tricks. He's for them on baseball teams and also goes for colored comedians. He raves about Sammy Davis, not because of color but because of ability. Davis sings, dances and impersonates white stars so great. If you close your eyes you can almost see them. My father says, "That boy's an artist."

No, my father's not a racist like some around this town. One night when there was Ku Klux Klan stuff on evening TV, Dad switched it off. "That's not the way to be American," he said. He just doesn't want coloreds for neighbors. He has practical reasons. He says, "I'm putting my life into paying off this home. Now who's going to buy it at a price that will get us something equal to what we have? Where do we go? Coloreds bring down property values."

Mom told him times are changing and lots of blacks are famous and even become mayors of big cities. He still feels the same.

"I don't want them next door to me. I stay with my own kind. What's the matter, don't they like each other? Every night on the news all I see is slums and reports about *crack* and *murder*. Do I try to live next door to them?"

Suddenly, once again, my sick feeling came over me. A lot of times I get real dizzy, like I'm about to faint. Right in the middle of his argument, I wanted to scream, and it wasn't about other people. It was about how he never got mad enough over what happened to me, his very own daughter. And he won't allow any talk about it. Whenever I try, it turns into a fight. Are a house and new neighbors more important than a person who is your child?

My uncle, Dad's brother, should not have been in this neighborhood, much less in our home. Okay, he's gone now. But nothing was right again, even after he left. One day, a long time ago, Mom walked in on me in my uncle's room. Is a kid nine years old supposed to know about bad sex stuff and how to protect herself? I wanted to tell. I tried to tell them how Uncle Ed was making me come to his room, asking me to bring a soda from the fridge. But I was afraid, ashamed, couldn't say it just right. Couldn't explain the things he did to me with his hands. There he'd be, stretched out almost naked on his bed. When I went in he'd pretend to be asleep. I knew he wasn't. I'd try to tiptoe away, and he'd call me back, hold my hand and I'd be, like, trapped.

"Uncle Ed, please, I have to go. There's your soda."

He'd hold my wrist and whisper, "Pop the lid for me, let's share it." He'd pat the side of the bed and smooth a place for me to sit.

I tried to beg out. "I think Mom wants me to go to the store."

I was scared to move until he'd say "Okay, my dear, run along." He never said it in a hurry. He squeezed my wrists together hard. "Your mother did not ask you to go to the store, did she?"

"No, sir."

"My darling Theodora, you don't want to be the kind of little girl who tells lies, do you?"

"No, sir."

"You know that I love you."

"I guess."

"I'm going to buy you a bike for your birthday. You want one, don't you?"

"I guess."

"If someone is good to you, don't you think it would be nice to be kind and grateful?"

"Yes, sir, but Mom and Dad—we don't kiss like this and we don't talk this way."

"Give me a small silent kiss and we'll keep it our secret. Theo dearest, darling, you make me do these things. It's all your fault. Take my hand. Now touch. Touch there. You're a naughty devil of an angel, you are. When you hold me I'm helpless."

"I want to go and see if Mom needs something from the store."

"Soon, but not yet. Say 'I'll stay, Uncle Ed.'"

"Yes, sir, Uncle Ed, I will." He made me put my hands on him. It was *not* my fault. And so Mom found us.

Sure, now Dad gets all worked up over who lives next door, and Mom's telling him about changing times. And I've never seen him so angry.

"Helen, shut up that ignorant talk about mayors and movie stars. We have to run the intruders out of the neighborhood!" Then he shook his finger in my face. "Theodora, when they move in, don't sit out back sunning yourself in a bikini like you're asking to be raped."

That did it. I got a dizzy spell again, sick to my stomach. It still happens, shrink or no shrink. I screamed, "Dad, why didn't you keep Uncle Ed away from me? Why didn't you run *him* out of the neighborhood?"

That made him furious. "I did, Theo. Look around, is he here? He's gone. I don't speak to my only brother on account of you. Isn't that enough? Ed loaned me the down payment on this house, and I threw him the hell out of it. And don't blame it all on him."

"Dad, I was a child."

"Why the hell were you always in his room?"

Mom coldly, quietly tore into him. "Don't say that to her. She was and she still is a child. She's our child, and Ed was an adult."

He cried. "I'm sorry, Theodora, I didn't mean it. I'm going crazy."

But he sat up half the night making angry phone calls to old neighbors about the new ones. I went to my room and vomited. What does he care?

Over five years gone and there is never a day that I really forget. Yes, Uncle Ed's way off in California, maybe with another little "secret love." No, he doesn't have to take out-of-town bus trips for therapy like I do. He didn't have to have his insides examined by a doctor. Mom and Dad had been *pleased* with the doctor's *good* report. "The girl is still a virgin. She'll be okay." Good report. So what? Well, that was then and now is now. No more of me being scared of men, you can bet on that. I'm going to press charges against that body grabber Rex Hardy for *attempted rape*, even if nobody else in the world will help me to do it.

Last night Dad clamped his hands on my shoulders, almost to the bone, and tried to shake my head off. "Leave the Rex Hardy thing alone. I believe you. I'm sure the guy got way out of line. But I'm protecting you, Theo. Do you want your mental and medical history paraded through open court? Do you need lawyers questioning you in public? Do you want more physicals to find out if you are or are not a virgin? They put girls through that. Child abuse charges can be hell. Damn it, as for your Uncle Ed, it's over. When something dies, at least let's bury it. You can be attacked once, but twice gets suspicious! Who do you have for witnesses? Who will speak up for you? Jonathan Barnett and Tyrone Tate? One's a faggot and the other's a nigger. I will not let you make a public spectacle of yourself. What's your charge? Assault and *attempted* rape? The courts are not interested in what *almost* happens to people!"

"Daddy, you don't believe me?"

Surprise—Mother went to backing him up. Hugging me but agreeing with him. "Theo, darling, it's not a question of belief. You don't want public scars on your name. A few years from now you'll understand."

How can they be for me and against me? "Daddy, you don't even care what Rex Hardy did?"

He said, "I care, but the only thing I can do is kill him. Theo, I'd *rather* kill him than see you in court. Most people manage to keep family secrets. I can't let you hurt yourself. Some day you'll want to marry. Why should a bride drag a court scandal down the aisle with her?"

"Daddy, what happens to Rex Hardy?"

I hated to see my mother cry. She's so little. She said, "Maybe he'll be sent away, he'll move. Maybe you'll never see him again, ever."

Good for him and Uncle Ed. They just vanish. I'd like to run away myself, but I can't. I just *won't*! I told my father, "I don't need you to kill anyone. I'm going to take Hardy to court. You'll see. I'll protect myself. A girl shouldn't need to depend on anybody to do it for her!"

6 Susan Tate

I DON'T GIVE A DAMN ABOUT JONATHAN BARNETT or Theodora Lynn or anybody else in this simple-ass town, except my brother Tyrone. I'm walking around feeling like a thief. A sick thief. Tyrone was beginning to get into the rhythm of Mini High and Minitown before trouble started. But all I saw, see and feel are bad vibes. One thing—it sure is chilly at Mini High. During classroom changes, that's when you find out where you stand with the others. The girls talk while they close their notebooks and prepare to rush madly through corridors on the way to gym, science or wherever. The most popular ones have others following behind them, listening to every word they say.

One girl named Karen is so popular she can hardly get to where she's going, 'cause there'll be maybe six or seven groupies making over her. "Karen, what are you *doing* after math?" And, "Karen don't forget my *party* on Saturday." Or, "Karen, remember we're going to the Zig-Zag Clothes Emporium, *you promised*." And Karen laughs and throws back answers by the dozen and loves every minute of being alive.

It's like they're all enjoying a grand excitement without anything big really going on. Electric sparks seem to fly through the air because everyone is liking themselves and glad to be in with popular people who let them be a part of their gladness. I was a popular person like that back in Crown Heights, Brooklyn.

Next in line, after big-time pop girls, come the in-between happy ones. They walk along together by twos or threes, groaning about teachers who gave them a B when they think they should rate a B+. Sometimes they're telling about trips they had last summer or buying another new dress or just about trivia. Anything at all. But they're very happy busy about it.

One day, tired of being alone, I hung around the fringes, listening to the big-time pops. They were giggling about how boys play tricks on girl students. Sort of an initiation thing. Grabbing them for a kiss and a fast feel in the clothing closet. Once someone doused the lights in the science lab and the last one out got a thrill-scare. A surprise boy in the dark. He felt her up, top and bottom, in a familiar, snatchy way. However, after that she was accepted as a genuine member of the pop crowd. I edged closer into the circle and said, "Gee, I sure am glad to know about it. I'll be careful and watch my step."

They exchanged amazed looks. Then this tall, curly-headed girl named Thelma said, "But none of the boys will ever do that to *you*."

I got their message. I am to remain an outsider.

Another student smiled, shrugged her shoulders and said, "Don't worry, Susan, you're safe." Then they walked away whispering. I didn't want to be grabbed by anybody. But I did not appreciate their attitude.

A pretty one named Shelly ran back and stammered out a kind of worried message. "Susan, I hope nobody—I mean none of us hurt your feelings."

I answered smoothly, "No way, Shelly. Only people I *care* about can hurt me."

She stood there looking silly until one in the bunch called her. "Shelly, are you coming?"

As for the rest of the female students, there are a few real loners. They read bulletin boards *alone.* Go off at lunchtime to eat a sandwich and read a book *alone.* They're deep into being brain-busy and don't have time for anyone. Well, that's great, hooray for real loners. But it's no fun if you have to pretend you're one. I try to pass for a loner, okay? I walk around trying to look like I'm alone on purpose.

But now the light freeze around here is stone cold like an iceberg. So someone attempted to rape that Theodora Lynn. Well, she's some of everything, which means maybe she's nothing in particular. One time she's a loner, then next she's with the brainies, then mostly alone again. Not one thing or another. She would have to be my next-door neighbor. Last week she stopped, like, to talk to me, and I walked on. Next time I decided to speak to her, and she walked on. Everything is—weird.

The one boy who tried to make a play for me, Spencer Reese, was one nobody else seems to want. In compu-class I'd look up and there he'd be, staring at me. Once he winked. I'm not at all interested, but at least a wink meant somebody thought I was attractive, maybe. One day, after that, he was walking in one direction in the corridor and I in the opposite. No one else around, okay? As he passed, he grinned, reached out and grabbed me down in a personal place and said, "I am a chocoholic," and kept going.

I called after him, "You're a dirty racist cracker son of a bitch." I thought of telling Tyrone, but then he'd have to fight him and maybe some of his friends too, if Spencer has any.

Yesterday as I left English lit on my way to science, I was in the middle of a mad rush on the down stairwell. Someone shoved my back and sent me plunging headlong. I fell into people and grabbed the handrail. A girl in front yelled, "Hey, watch it!" The crowd behind me went rushing by. Spencer Reese was among them. I'm sure he's the one who pushed, but he kept going, looking, like, innocent. I was wearing my baby-doll shoes, and one button broke off. My hand picked up a splinter from dragging along the rail. Did any of those others turn back to help me? You better believe they did not. My body and my feelings were hurt. That's where Jonathan Barnett found me, alone.

"What's the matter, Susan?"

"Somebody pushed me."

"Who did it?"

"I don't know."

"Are you hurt?"

"Not much."

"What should we do about it?"

"From now on I'll make sure to be the last one down and also watch my back."

He tried to help me up but I wouldn't move. "Want to see the nurse? Would you like me to walk you to your next class?"

I answered no twice. I didn't want to go to anybody's class. He wouldn't leave me alone. Just sat there patting my shoulder till I broke down crying. "I've got a problem and nobody to talk to."

"You can talk to me, Susan."

"I can't."

"Because I'm an instructor?"

"Maybe."

"Because I'm white?"

"Get off my case, will you?"

"You have to trust somebody, Susan. I promise not to tell about your problem. I won't tell anybody."

I looked straight into his eyes and kind of believed him, but believing or not, I was no way ready to spill my guts. "Look, Barnett, here's a problem. What if you could save someone's life? Someone you hate, would you save the person?"

He got very big eyed. "Save someone's life? How?"

"Well, save them from a disease maybe, or deep disgrace. Suppose I had, like, a new pill that could cure them—but I wouldn't let them have it."

"Susan, you'd have to hate awfully hard to be that mean."

"The way people treat me I can hate that hard. I might even gladly destroy that lifesaving pill."

"But if it worries you to do it, if it makes you unhappy . . ." I changed the subject to explain my feelings.

"My Uncle Kwame went to West Africa last year. He visited Ghana and saw this museum called Elmina Castle. It's where slave traders once upon a time locked Africans in stone dungeons without drinking water or even toilet places. They were locked up to wait for slave ships to bring them here to America, okay? Some made plans to escape, but they mostly failed because another slave always told on the rest. An informer. A finger pointer. He told on others to make things easier for himself. All I'm saying is you'd better not trust anyone if you can't even trust your own people, right?"

Barnett sadly shook his head. "That's been true throughout history. It happens among all groups. There will always be traitors."

I cut him off from his damned easy smooth answers. What has he ever had to go through? None of his history books even contain my history. So I dumped on him. "My Uncle Kwame told how there's now an altar in one of the slave rooms at Elmina Castle. His guide explained that just a few years ago an African woman had a terrible dream: a spirit voice told her a shrine must be built by today's Africans, to beg forgiveness because of those traitors turning against their own, making money off selling them into slavery. So the people obeyed her and built that shrine to display the rusty chains, shackles and whipping posts. Today they burn candles on that altar to remind us how cruel some can be to others. Uncle Kwame says that right now too many of our own are still cruel to each other."

"Susan," he said in his stubborn way, "that's not an exclusive thing. It didn't happen just to your people. I've had someone close to me, of my race, turn on me. He betrayed me. It hurts, I know."

Barnett is a lucky white boy. Lucky I didn't wind up and hit him one square in the eye. No matter what awful thing happens to others, white folks always say they have it just as bad or worse. Kind of like saying, "It's tough all over." That kind of attitude. "Look," I said, "let's change the subject back to now. What if you could save someone you hate—would you do it?"

"You mean someone of a different race? What difference would that make?"

He still has that picky kind of racism buried deep down. Whatever happens to me he's looking for a way to dispute me about it. They refuse to see anything special about being me. I told him, "Barnett, four hundred years of slavery is a no-fair way to start out in a new world." When his mouth flew open to dispute some more, I cut him off. "Bring me no tales about immigrants who came here poor and rose to the top. Poor immigrants had the right to ride trains, streetcars, buses and sit where they wanted to sit even before they ever became citizens. We black citizens could not do that until Reverend Martin Luther King, Jr., turned it around. Now, answer me this—would you ask Jews to forget the Holocaust 'cause it also happened to other people?"

"No, I wouldn't ask that."

"Well, if you do, they're not going to go for it. And I for one don't blame them, okay?"

"And I don't blame them, Susan."

"Then don't blame me! I had one grandfather that I never even met because he died over in Germany fighting World War II. And here, in the U.S.A., while he was on his way to boot training in the South, he had to ride in the back of the bus—Jim Crow. And right here, in the U.S.A., German prisoners of war did not ever have to do that because they were white, okay? My Uncle Kwame told me that I am a very special person. One part of a very special people, going through a lot of mean, special things every day. So don't you tell me how to paddle my canoe unless you're in the same boat. Like my uncle says, everything that's been dropped on our shoulders, others try to discuss it away for us like it's nothing."

"Susan, being different is a fine thing. It *can* be a fine thing."

"I know that. I'm different . . . and I'm proud of it. Uncle Kwame said just this morning, 'Don't let those other people force you to rebuild yourself in their image. Some are so vain they think God is exactly like them and the rest of us are God's mistakes.'"

He looked real sad and said, "Susan, everyone should have an Uncle Kwame in their family."

"Everybody can't be that lucky," I said. "What do

you know about having it tough? You're only a kid and have a job teaching other kids. How did that happen? I bet you knew someone who smoothed the way for you."

"Come to think of it, Susan, it was kind of that way."

At that point Mr. Lampkin, my math teacher, peeked down the stairwell and got on Barnett about us being where we were. Didn't talk like one teacher to another. Shook his finger and gave a scolding. "Mr. Barnett, sitting on the steps and fraternizing is out of order. That student is supposed to be in class. Don't you think we have enough trouble going on without asking for more?"

Barnett didn't hop up and move. I liked that. He said, "Yes, Mr. Lampkin, we sure do have enough trouble. I agree." He said it sternly like dismissing an intruder.

I didn't pay that math man any attention either. So he took off. Then I started to go. Barnett pulled me back. "Susan, hey, wait. What about that person you could save but won't?"

I had almost forgotten about Theodora Lynn. "Oh, it was just kind of a make-believe problem. Anyway, maybe nobody can save anyone except themselves. Maybe each of us should just look out for number one, right?"

"Come on, Susan, do we really want to build that kind of world?"

"That's the kind it is, Mr. Barnett. We don't have to build it."

I wondered why I had told him about Uncle Kwame's

trip to West Africa and about racism stuff, spilling out my guts. Well, anyway Jonathan Barnett doesn't seem particularly white. He's more like just a plain person. Before you know it you can become trusting and confiding, if you don't watch out.

I walked away before he could ask me anything else. But I liked him a little better than when we started. Everybody white isn't exactly Spencer Reese . . . I guess. As for that Mr. Lampkin, he is old enough to show some respect for youth. I bet he never shook his finger at Principal Mitchell.

7 Jonathan Barnett

THE PHONE HAS BEEN QUIET FOR A HALF HOUR. Ignorant Mr. Anonymous is giving me a short rest from his repeated, hateful, nasty message. "Lousy faggot, nigger lover, friend of a whore. Speak against Rex Hardy and we'll hang your AIDS ass on the outskirts of town." Wow. When I'm alone at night and getting those calls! Hey, I can hear Landlady Trale walking overhead, soft footsteps back, forth and around. She moves almost as quietly as Lataweeze. Must be wearing felt bedroom slippers. Reminds me of my mother.

At home, in the house, Mom wears sneakers. It's hard to know Mom's there until she's almost on top of you. An easy walker. Thinking back, I was only eight the day she found me in her room, my head buried in lace. "Jonathan, what are you doing?"

I almost jumped out of my skin and through the cloud of white material. She had bought nine yards of it to send to a friend in Cleveland. Somebody or other getting married.

"Jonathan, what are you doing?"

What was I doing? Well, she had sent me upstairs to get that package. I lifted the paper bag by the wrong end, and out tumbled the lace like a waterfall, all over the floor. I picked it up and tried to fold it flat again. The softness brushed against my cheek. I held it there, liked the feel of it.

"Jonathan, what's the matter?"

"Nothing, it's just pretty."

I felt ashamed, like, caught at a wrong thing, hugging lace. "I'm not doing anything," I protested. Again the material dropped to the floor.

"Jon," she said, "boys don't play with dress goods."

"I wasn't playing, only holding it."

"You don't need to hold it." She spoke abruptly, then changed to a gentler tone. "Maybe you ought to spend time with your father."

"I do."

"I mean spend *more* time with him and less around me."

"Why?"

She led me over to her dressing table. "It was thoughtful of you to do this yesterday, but I don't want you arranging my nail polish and perfume. Boys shouldn't concern themselves with such things."

I had heard her complain about it looking a mess. I thought she would be pleased that I had straightened it. But I had made her unhappy. "Mother, I won't do it again."

After that Dad began to talk to me a lot. "Hey, son, did I ever mention that my grandfather used to do oil painting? As a hobby, of course. You'd never meet a manlier guy. You remind me of him. You're a pretty rugged little fellow also."

I tried to please them. I made the softball and track teams and I didn't look like the worst athlete out there, either. They were proud of me, they said.

When I was thirteen they bought the country place on Turnabout Mountain. Jim, Fern and I were a happy threesome, but she couldn't go with us because, being a girl, there were certain things she wasn't allowed to do—like spending the night with boys. But Jim and I hung around her house a lot when we weren't off on our own. After all, she did have her computer and also an eight-track hi-fi. Looking back, I'd say we were all as happy as we needed to be. Childhood wasn't just awful. It was A-OK most of the time.

"Hey, Jon, eeooow!" That was Jim's call that meant "It's on. Let's do something." We roughhoused a lot. He was a right guy on the basketball court. Couldn't handle math too well. I used to tease him with my grandfather's old joke, "Bet you can't count over twenty, 'cause you'd run out of fingers and toes." One Christmas Fern and I chipped in and bought him a $10 calculator. It was an el-cheapo, no-name brand. But it sure figured numbers better than he could.

Turnabout was different than in town. Jim held out a hand to pull me over the rocky places. I did the same for him when I was the one on higher ground. Sometimes we kept on holding hands for no reason at all, just walking along arms swinging. In town we didn't help one another over rough spots. And there was never any handholding. Without saying, we knew that it looked dumb. Turnabout was like another world.

Some crazy storms happened up there. One night turned into an electrical blockbuster. We did the right things, stayed in away from trees and turned off the power. Suddenly out of the storm clouds came thunder, then lightning and high wind. Everything going on except rain. We huddled together, away from windows, and tried to tell jokes. But a mountain storm can make you shut up or scream. Thundering sound and big bright crackling, lightning fingers threw us into a state of grinning fear. Spots of electricity balls jumped around out on the porch. They bounced and rippled along, bright, crooked and whining like a scene from some crazy movie about outer space. Zigzag electric fingers leaped from black clouds and shot down, searching for us. A tree crashed about a quarter mile away, but sounded as if headed straight for the cabin roof. All that action brought on a hard hail storm. One nugget, size of a golf ball, crashed through the window and split the floor. Rain started as heavier thunder grumbled. Water came pouring down and over the shack. Outside became a roaring river. One tough rain. We used every pot, pail, bucket and barrel to catch the flood streaming through the roof. We wrapped one sleeping bag in the other and shoved them in a closet without exchanging a word. An emergency can educate you into silent cooperation—but fast. Soaking wet and fighting back with the help of a broom and a mop, we swept puddles out to the porch. In less than an hour the storm stopped. The night turned cold, moonless, pitch dark and dead quiet, except for the sound of dripping water. That outer sleeping bag was soggy wet. We placed the other on top of a shower curtain, scrambled out of our wet clothes and, with teeth chattering, we hopped in the sack, clinging and holding on to each other until warmth enveloped us. A lot of fumbling and intimate touching went on. Maybe we'd been heading toward it for a long time—with or without a storm.

In the morning, we talked too loud, too much and too long about nothing in particular. After that night I was close to Jim, even though he sat on the far side of our classroom and lived on the other side of town. He was the first person I loved. We never discussed the relationship.

A year later Jim's mother married a man who was here visiting from England. That was the end. They went overseas. Jim was gone. That hurt for a long time. We wrote each other almost every day for nearly a year. I slacked off when he began mentioning a "smashing" girl. Her name kept coming up in his letters. I got the message. Soon he stopped writing. Jim was growing into manhood, in love with a girl. I was a passing phase in his life, but he had been much more than that in mine. Through him I became known to myself, and soon there was another experience, and another. I was not then, and am not now, comfortable with who and what I am.

It was disturbing when gays, in passing, seemed to recognize me without introduction. Eye contact. Here and there. Now and then. They looked puzzled when I turned away from their unspoken messages. But they knew me and—I knew them. The boys and the men. Some were kind and looked the other way. Others seemed to silently scream through a sarcastic smile, "Hey, Queen, who do you think you're kidding? I know you. Welcome to the club."

Sometimes I gave in. Mostly I tried to drop out. I didn't admire myself or too many of the others. But they were there, reaching out to me and once in a while I reached. I tried to turn away from gay life for good reason. Jonathan Barnett had to be more than someone's lover, more than a misfit. I've always wanted to please my parents and to be pleased with myself. Seems it just can't be done, no matter how I try.

A full turn on of this gas fireplace and I would not have to worry about anything anymore. Not Mrs. Trale, my father or mother, other people named anonymous, public opinion, Theodora Lynn's problems or Harper Mead. I'd be out, free. Maybe courage in general is what I lack. Now that's the gift for the boy who has everything, more courage. It takes nerve to exit, but now I know it takes even more nerve to live and face the daily music.

8 Rex Hardy

MY BIGGEST MISTAKE IS CARING TOO MUCH. Being a pal to my students. Too ready to share their mixed-up young lives. I even extended the welcoming hand to instructor Jonathan Barnett, and my reward is a mental kick in the heart. I tried to help a young nobody who's now ready to ruin the rest of my life. Another thing, why did Principal Mitchell ever ask me to give *special attention* to that troublesome Reese boy? Spencer is annoying, his dad is sickening, a first-class bigot. So the father makes the son sick. Why do I play doctor? Because I like kids, I guess. The boy seems to admire me, though he doesn't get along with others. Against my better judgment, I took him under my wing. It's hard to do everything right. Spence takes over and tries to make me follow. Why do I play with children? Foolishly, I always place myself in their hands.

Spence asked me to do something or other just a few moments before the crazy thing happened. I was busy between a raggedy cheerleader practice and compu-

confusion. I cut him off and went to steal a smoke in the cleaning closet. Soon Theodora stalked in behind me. I don't know why, but I kissed her. She was bumbling around looking for something. I only meant to . . . what did I mean? It was just a fun thing—until she screamed, now my life is almost over. What in hell was I doing locked in a dark closet with a hysterical girl? I only put my hand over her mouth to stop the noise. She struggled. That rattled me. We were body to body—I don't remember too much after that. I would not knowingly hurt Theodora or anyone else. It was a mix-up, a mistake. I am now and I've always been a dedicated teacher under any and all circumstances . . . just about.

Spencer Reese had told me, the day before, that he was going to play a trick on Theo. Planned to set her up in some childish way. I should have put a stop to any plan he had. But I've always thought it an honor to share a kid's secrets. I guess I'm just too proud about being the adult selected to share confidences—too proud about being *included*. I have a fine wife, Amy, and two healthy kids, Rex Jr., nine, and Rita, six. We're buying an old-fashioned, small three-bedroom house. I'm very grateful for what little we have—and ready to fight tooth and nail to keep it.

Amy works part-time as a saleslady at the shopping mall. I'm now legally advised to stay out of school on *sick* leave. I sure feel *sick*. Until a few days ago I was routinely teaching at Mini High and moonlighting on Saturdays. Giving tennis lessons at the country club. Like a whole lot of other Americans, I work extra outside hours just to live a decent, simple life. I don't envy anybody, but we all want a few extras for our families. To be comfortable. Have a roof over our heads, and enough set aside for a rainy day—providing it doesn't turn into a typhoon.

I work even harder for free than for pay. I'm a chronic time and energy giver. I've donated services above and beyond every call of duty. "Will someone volunteer to . . ." When Principal Mitchell starts off like that, my hand is up and I'm standing before giving the matter further thought. I'm a student advisor, without the title or the pay, a gratis public relations man, and a self-appointed fund-raiser, forever rounding up support from the business community.

Yes, I gave a hands-out welcome to Jonathan Barnett. I was even kind of glad to see a new male instructor. The other men teaching here seem to adjust to female leadership with no evident discomfort. They don't care who's over their heads, as long as the paycheck's delivered on time. Don't get me wrong, I truly admire women . . . who are womanly. But it does get me to watch some of them taking over the educational system. High school teaching, like intermediate and elementary, is fast becoming too much of a woman's thing.

I tried to crack a joke in a teachers' meeting. "There was once a good old Chinese custom, a woman's place used to be two steps behind her man . . ." Miss Weldon, another teacher, cut in before I could make my point. She made me apologize for telling an "*anti-woman*" joke. The others backed her up. Nobody knows how to laugh anymore. There was no comfort about it at home either. My own wife said I was wrong. How about that? Murderers are walking around free while I have to apologize about a little joke, a friendly remark.

Physical ed, my job, used to have something to do with being male. That's healthy. But it's on the way out. These women today are not helpless, clinging vines. I've seen gals pump iron and perform a bench workout that would leave me breathless. They'll bust a gut, die trying to outdo a man.

One thing I'll say for myself though, I never lag too far behind the times. I've initiated more new programs than anyone in this school, including the big Ms. herself, Principal Mitchell. But believe you me this school is a jungle. After I get things going, someone always moves in to rip me off, steal credit and take the bows.

A while back I started a hard-rock cheerleader section. Our school band is now up to playing the best of the Top 40 tunes. And the cheerleaders are pepper-hot. Five great singers back them up, while Theodora Lynn lead-dances in front of the front line. Say what you will, fresh and way out as she is, she has the real right stuff. Nobody can catch up with her. She is one naturally charged up person. I edited the tired old rah-rahs out of our school song. It now goes "Win baby win, never say die, mow 'em down baby, for Mini Mini High. Mini Mini High." Then the cheer gals run in kicking and jumping through a fast flipping, shake-it thing, while the band blasts into a funk-rock arrangement of Sousa's "Stars and Stripes Forever." Precision. Teamwork. I added a few muscle-flexing boys to the sides of the cheer section. They wear red satin jocks and helmets. The guys glisten from head to foot with suntan oil and change poses while the girls, in blue and white bikinis, shake red rhinestone fringe, feathers and glittery streamer ribbons on gold sticks. Talk about full-color action. The routine screams!

The first time Minitown played basketball against Big City High the crowd went mad. We won 77 to 70 and swept the press. Principal Mitchell loved it. So what did she do? Brought in a woman choreographer to take over and re-direct *my* cheerleader program. The new laid-back gal gave the band a few extra fancy moves. All she did was smear a dab of icing on my cake. The results were—let's say maybe slicker. Everybody knows I was the one who got Bentley's Department Store to donate tailor-made sequin band uniforms. And they sure came over real splashy-dashy, and dandy-fine gaudy. When credit time came, the lady choreographer walked off with two live TV interviews, a front-page picture and a double-column newspaper article. She was hailed as the "mover and shaker" behind Mini High's "unique and innovative" cheer section. Principal Mitchell was elated. Rip-off people crush you body and soul. Ask me. Today's password is snatch and steal, wheel and deal.

Take this computer program, for instance. I dug the foundation. Laid the groundwork. Studied the basics and planned out how I'd carry my beginners at a pace or two behind me. Little did I know I was setting up for somebody else. Mrs. Mitchell claimed she was afraid I couldn't get into word processing *fast* enough. She moved to bring in some out-of-town girl. When the gal changed her mind, instead of stepping aside saying, "No thank you," like a lady, she strong-armed a way for this Barnett to step in and take over. Seems the boy's so smart he can afford to delay college entrance for a year. Well, maybe he can also pass the finals and grab a degree without attending college at all. Such things can happen.

Talk about sprinkling salt in my wounds. Principal Mitchell asked me to make him feel welcome. "You're so good at that, Hardy," she had the nerve to say. "And you are his elder." She gave me two school cafeteria passes to pull off the welcoming reception. I refused them.

"No thanks, Mrs. Mitchell. I think I'll take him around to the Wayward Garden."

"We have no funds for that, Mr. Hardy."

"I don't either, but I'll borrow on my credit card."

The "Garden" has plants hanging from the ceiling. Perhaps "Wayward" is because they also have a liquor and beer license. Well, I couldn't take Barnett to our zooville school cafeteria and maintain that good old elder image. I don't like to fight dripping ketchup pumps, mustard jars, steam tables and nonstop noise. Out of my own pocket I took my successor to the Wayward Garden.

My thirty-nine years must have seemed like a hundred to him. It's not easy to let a boy know who's the man while helping him to replace yourself. But I definitely wanted him to get the right message. He looked like a younger member of that tireless hang-in-there breed—the *me generation*. They don't know a damned thing about rejection. He sat facing me, wearing gray casuals and a confident smile. I gave him a well thought out ten-minute explanation of my successful efforts to start our Compu-One program. I laid it on pretty heavy so he'd clearly understand who was handing him a gift.

He cut in. "Mr. Hardy, I appreciate all that you've done and will welcome any help you can offer. After a semester or two I'll be gone and you'll be back in charge again. I mean, well, Mrs. Mitchell told me that you'll be auditing my course."

I wanted to slap him hard, rip his head off, send it rolling across the marble-patterned floor. I wanted to see his sassy blood flow like the Red Sea. Talk about a snide remark. "I'll be gone and you'll be *back* in charge again." Talk about swallowing an insult.

I laughed, shrugged and hated myself for trying to talk young, while giving him a weak snow job. "Right on the button, Barnett. Let's change the subject. Did you leave someone brokenhearted by coming to Minitown?"

He flinched. His eyes widened. Ha, I had pinched a secret nerve. He quietly pulled himself together. "Huh?"

"Isn't there a gorgeous gal somewhere waiting?"

"Oh, that. Well, I'll see her some weekends."

"A fast game of tennis helps keep the mind off the girly stuff, right?"

That was supposed to get a laugh. It didn't. I teach the facts of life to youngsters. After all, these are sexily dangerous times. In my work, we're all surrounded daily by young bodies dressing and undressing—a lot of sweaty togetherness. Well, I've learned how to handle that. Ignore them, except for giving a sportsman's pat. A gentle casual slap on the bottom. Just enough to say, "You did well." Pat, slap. "You did well."

At home, Amy and I, we get in so weary. Dead tired and for good reason. Best we can manage these days is a weak hug and a quick kiss. Besides the regular work and the extra jobs, there's always more to do. Look after the kids, the house, that thirsty lawn, and make out the bills. By the time we get home from church—the weekend's over. Too little time and too much to do. Sex, at home or school, is a thought that seldom crosses my mind.

How great it would be if Amy and I could go back to the days before things went kinda wrong in the first place. Once, just once, a malicious teenager, a sick-head, accused me of trying to make her go all the way. That was heartache time for me and Amy.

Four years ago in a teenage summer camp I was counselor. A lie like that girl told, even though cleared up, stands between a man and his wife. I was completely exonerated, and rightly so. We talked it out every kind of way. But scandal isn't good for a marriage. Poor Amy.

Barnett sharply raised his voice and scattered my thoughts. "I don't go in for tennis, Mr. Hardy." Sure took his time answering.

"Well, I also jog a couple of miles or so Saturday mornings with a few of the boys. You're welcome to come along."

"And I don't jog."

He'd eaten only one-third of his meal and was busy shoving the rest around on the plate. I remembered thinking it's not like a normal young man to order an omelette for lunch. He pushed his dessert around also. Some sort of *Spanish* pudding—*flan*. A very strange boy. Last year we had a Mexican kid on track team—but he ate hamburgers and hot dogs like a regular fellow. Fit right in.

I tried to explain the state of our school and its people, Principal Mitchell, the teachers, and the students. I told him about Theodora and her offbeat ways. "She's a bit slow at times, Barnett, but gorgeous gals don't have to be extra brilliant, when Mother Nature's been so very kind." He gave no answer on that. Not too outgoing at all. I explained another special student, Spencer Reese. "Now he's busy in a restless way and can be headstrong. Even gets mean at times. A good boy, just disruptive to get attention. Tries too hard to be like his father, who's anti everything. And there are also two new students, a Negro youngster, fourteen, and his fifteen-year-old sister. Some of our local citizens don't like blacks coming in. Most people around here are more or less friendly. But some have a strained attitude toward certain other people. Those unlike the rest of us. Well that's to be expected, I suppose."

"How do you feel about that subject, Mr. Hardy?" His question had a raw edge to it.

"Well, we're all kind of different one way or another, wouldn't you say? Mrs. Mitchell, our principal, definitely wants all treated fairly and—"

He cut me off kind of abruptly. "Thanks for the lunch, sir."

He never liked me, right from the start. I tried to be nice to him but he wouldn't allow it, kept fending me off. I don't want to harm him, neither did his *friend* Harper Mead. But if that Mead guy hadn't given me a scandal weapon, I'd be up the dirty creek without a paddle, a helpless pawn between a come-on girl, a faggot and a cocky Negro. I don't believe in blackmail. But as Rocky says, "A man's gotta do what a man's gotta do." I can't see my wife hurt again. Amy has suffered enough. I'm not going to allow anybody to hurt her or me either—that also goes for our kids. When it comes to my children, I'm ready to die.

9 Lila Barnett

JON SHOULD HAVE CONTINUED HIS EDUCATION. He seems perfectly rational, but now these calls from Minitown about a teacher trying to rape a girl student. And Jon about to be a witness. I'm glad he told us. We have always encouraged him to confide. But his honesty is getting to be too damned much. My son has his own problems, why must he bother with those other people?

I'm trying to think back to see what I did wrong, if anything. Is this homosexual thing really the whole problem? No, not a problem, I'll call it an isolated event. But events can sure hurt when they strike home. Cal and I never saw any homosexual tendencies in Jonathan—not definitely. I don't see any now. Maybe we refuse to see it. We're only human. We can be wrong.

Being an only child might not have been a good thing for Jon. But lots of other people are onlies and they don't become—oh, I don't know. Anyway, he is different. It's awfully hard on Calvin. A normal father probably feels more pain than a mother about a son turning out gay.

Yes, Cal really hurts. I try to talk with him, but we stop too soon to get started.

Jon's *lifestyle,* as they call it these days, is abhorrent to me. My mind keeps spinning like a windmill. In the middle of the night I wrestle with feelings, trying to find out exactly what I truthfully think and how to put it into words for Jon and Cal. I can't.

Three years ago a close, good friend confided in me. Her nephew had come out of the closet. She was grieving for herself, her sister and for him. My friend Dolores is a strong family person. Italian family at that. I think Italians have great regard for the tough, solid macho image. Well, Dolores and I—we lunched at the Willow Inn. Became watery eyed and managed to find our way back to a little unstrained laughter. She was grateful for my comforting assurances. I gave good advice. "At least life goes on. Differences make the world. We can't stop caring or withhold our love from a loved one because they're somehow different." Of course, we never solved anything. Her brother-in-law wouldn't even allow his son to come back in the house. But our getting together did help us. We both felt enlightened by honestly facing, discussing and considering the bare facts. Oh, that day is now so well remembered.

The Willow Inn is done in blue, yellow and gray. It's decorated with flowers and there's a frosted candle lamp at each table. They have real linen and crystal. One large central chandelier softly gleams amber light on the diners. Waiters and waitresses are neatly smart in yellow jackets and blue pants, all dressed alike. They call it *unisex*. A tiresome expression. Waiters with hair so long you can barely tell them from the girls. The food is good and ambiance is quite pleasant. A mirrored wall reflects the mahogany-and-brass bar in the next room. There was a pleasant hum of conversation mixed with the clinking and ringing of silverware and glass. Almost sounded orchestrated.

We discussed the word *gay*. Dolores said, "That's a silly way to describe any human being. It seems to imply a perpetual state of mirth." Gay, to me, suggests a pastoral fantasy of wood nymphs, leaping through green fields, chasing butterflies.

We both managed to summon up a minimal respect for the term homosexual. At least homo sounds manly. We definitely agreed that everyone in the world should have the right to be themselves, no matter what others might think.

But now I know it feels damned different when the gay one is your very own child. Yes, Dolores came to me then, but I sure can't go to her or any other outsider about Jon's problem. The hurt is too deep to share, too close to my heart. Anyway, that was her nephew, Jon is my *son*.

That day three years ago I found more understanding for a stranger than I can now find for my own child. What to do? Try to fake understanding when I don't understand? Cal and I have always had a solidly sensible, decent concerned attitude about social problems. We are against racism and child abuse. We're for women's rights. And we also have always definitely believed in the rights of homosexuals and lesbians. I once sent a contribution to help a college pay for a gay rights seminar. But this thing is entirely unexpected. This is *my* son. First things first. How could he have been attracted to such a person as that Harper Mead? Preferring males to females is problem enough. But why that particular male? What a cruel and small act to call Jonathan's parents and *tell* on him. The lowest form of *snitching,* that's what I call it. Anyway, he's older than Jonathan. I bet he led him astray. I'm glad I'm not his mother, poor woman.

I am proud that Jon dropped everything and came back home to face and comfort us. Cal and I—we decided to be kind and thoughtful about the problem. Not to even mention it for a while. Just laugh, have fun and act natural. Our first hope is that we're dealing with a passing phase. However, we're mature enough to know that some phases don't easily pass. I also hope we're not too worried about what others think. Our first concern has been, is now and always will be Jonathan.

In bed, in the dark I speak out my most secret worry. "Cal, what if he catches AIDS?"

"Lila, what if a heterosexual caught syphilis?"

"At least that's curable."

"Well, heteros also get AIDS. But it's less likely."

"I hate to think of how gays live."

"Well, all straights don't have conventional sex lives."

"Cal, your tit-for-tat comparisons don't make me feel a bit better."

"The same here."

"I love you, Cal."

"I love you. We both love our son, and he loves us."

Our arms were open when Jonathan arrived. His room was ready. Bed quilt turned back—the old faded green patchwork. All of Jonathan's favorite things were out—colored glass and stones collected from Turnabout Mountain, well-thumbed books on how to do this and how to do that. And the threadbare throw rug. He used to do his homework stretched prone on that very rug. We stuck to our plan. No prying for answers. Wait, wait a while to get to *that* subject. We were what we've always been, supportive parents. No person, particularly one named Harp, will ever be allowed to bend or break our family bond. We may not be entirely happy, but we're strong. We'll make ourselves happy. And every time he's home I'll ask Fern to dinner. Such a lovely girl.

10 Harper Mead

SO NOW I HEAR JON BARNETT HAS RUN AWAY from life again and managed to get himself into OPT—other people's troubles. The poor guy's about to go into drag, as Joan of Arc, to sacrifice himself for the sake of the greater society. The jerk can't handle his own problems, but is ready to star himself in the role of a do-gooder for others.

There is absolutely no fool like a *young* fool. Oh, but he can talk straight. Almost too straight for a guy who's bent. He's smart as a fox but has too much rabbit blood. Still too chicken about facing facts. I say whatever you are, *be* that. He's younger than I am but a lot smoother. He's a taker, I'm a giver. Boy, did he take me. I shared my apartment, my clothes, my equipment, my knowledge, my money, my life, myself. I taught him how to survive. He, like the rest of us, was born with some built-in smarts and quite a few stupids. They are pitted against one another. His stupids are winning the race.

He's chock-full of knowledge. If something's written down he's off and running. Math, science, world politics and computer crap. Scan a college catalog and you can bet he'd cover any subject as easily as dropping a chip on a bingo card. He's bright and smart in his own way—one brilliant square. It boggled my mind to see how he understands mechanical stuff. One day he glanced over the directions that came with a fifty-part do-it-yourself mail-order clock and said, "Got it." Jon threw the complicated mess together while I was still trying to figure out why screw B should fit into cog H when section A hadn't been mentioned yet.

My father works like that. "This gasket goes with that thingamajig." Even if he was bombed on two six-packs, he *knew*. Me, I can't make heads or tails out of written instructions. However, I'm never broke. I was born with a small gift for making a little money. As much of it as I really need. No more and no less. I found that out as a kid.

When a fifth grade teacher asked us to bring donations for the poor, most of us got it from home and that was that. Sure, I also got two bucks from my folks. But then I bought a box of twelve candy bars and sold ten of them as singles at thirty cents each. That left me with one buck and a couple of free bars for myself. So the poor got theirs and I made a little profit. I didn't learn that from any book. Soon other kids took a try at it but they didn't sell all of their candy, so they lost on the deal. The only thing I knew about candy is that folks like to eat it once you lead them to it. I made sure to be chomping and chewing on a bar while I was making my sale. When they saw me biting and smacking they became eager to buy. The name of the game is desire. Desire makes them grab for the product. It's hard to sell any idea unless the buyer is ready. That's salesmanship. It's a gift. I've got it. I'll never starve. Anything can be sold if you know how.

I wake up with schemes and ideas knocking on my head. Even though I didn't send for them. I do skip around from venture to venture, and haven't exactly settled on any one thing. As a kid, when I didn't have money to buy merchandise, I sold services. I shoveled snow and ran errands to get some cash on hand so I could wheel and deal. People buy stuff every day. We've got to. Right? We buy two things: first what we want and second what we need. That's seldom the same item. Your best bet is to get hold of what they want and set them up to buy it.

My smarts work. But my stupids shove me into cruddy situations. Sometimes I shoot off my mouth first and think later. Back with my folks in Middle City, couple of hundred miles west of New York, all I knew about the Big Apple was what I saw in movies and TV. But I sure wanted to be in New York City, to feel free, to show off and make a little money now and then. Truth is home got too slow and too hot. I had to get out fast. But somehow, some way, I always knew where I was going.

My blue-collar folks weren't born with silver spoons between their gums, but they did okay with the hardware store, selling nuts, bolts and pipe by the foot. That routine never turned me on. A life of peddling sandpaper and door locks, now really. But I learned to psych our customers into spending with a smile. At age fifteen my sales book jumped. At sixteen I talked Pop and Mom into stocking by mail order, designer wallpapers and paints, and a fancy line of decorative faucets, bathroom hardware. My pop could feel I still wasn't satisfied. For me the store was becoming a prison. Pulling, pushing, lifting and hauling is basically what my father understands. He's all muscle and strong as a bull. Solid steel, a reliable fix it guy.

I left home when I was half past seventeen. One evening, just before closing time, my father threw a letter on the store counter. Some jerk had sent him an unsigned note. Such cruddy characters ought to be maybe the only ones who get the electric chair. A sneak informer is always a few notches lower than what he's reporting. "Money-making Mead—Isn't it time you broke down and admit your son's a lousy fairy? You got to know he sneaks into the Pink Chameleon, two miles south on Highway One. Also slips out of town to gay bars. Straighten him or stop making a living off decent patriotic people. Anon."

Pop tried to shrug it off. "Some troublemaker enjoys sick jokes, right?"

The answer jumped out of my mouth and hit the air without my permission. "No, it's not a lie. I'm sorry you had to hear it from a person named Anon." That was all I got out. He slammed a hard oil-stained fist straight into my face. Three front teeth loosened and a piece of broken tooth cut through my upper lip. Warm salty blood filled my mouth. There I was on the floor, flat on my back. He picked me up and knocked me down again. My nose gushed blood and snot. That one minute of action left me with a battle scar under my left eye. I didn't defend myself. Talking back or raising a hand to my father was disrespectful—and also very risky.

A couple of years before, my older brother couldn't stand being pushed around so he cut out and joined the army. Enlisting is one way for an unhappy boy to leave home with honor. It's a hell of a lot easier to serve the country than to serve my father. The dentist wired two of my teeth back in place. One of them is still chipped, needs capping. Facially—that was a well-documented beating. I knew that the road to freedom had to be my next move—just walk away, say farewell to bondage.

Dad had a lot of bully in him when full of weekend grog. Liquor set his violent demon loose. During the work week he was mostly sober. But look out for Saturday afternoon through Sunday. He was a weekend drunk. He started with a few on the job on Friday night and slow follow-ups through Saturday into heavy on Sunday. He could never admit to being an alcoholic. He boasted, "I can *hold* my liquor." What he meant was he could tank up and still navigate without passing out on his butt. Boasting, boasting. "I work hard during the week. I deserve a little fun." On his knees over the toilet to throw up was often the bad end of his good time.

I used to joke with Mom. "Well, the old man sure tied one on yesterday."

She smiled, sad-like, and shook her head. "Well, your father works hard." She never spoke against him.

I remember him taking a swat at her now and then. When I jumped in between he walloped me. But still she never spoke against him. Wild weekends compensated him for hard labor. Lots of alcohol and open house for drop-in company. That was his release. His company, the regular fellows, he called them. His drinking buddies. Each boasted, "I don't let the grog interfere with my work. Work comes first. After the job, why not?" I kind of admired that. Never let pleasure interfere with the job. Secretly I added to it, and never let work interfere with regular pleasure.

I've seen champion elbow benders go through some hard drinking. When I was a little kid they used to spill a splash in my glass. "Drink up, boy, learn to hold it like a man." Dad liked me to drink. "A drop or two won't hurt you. Best place to learn to do it is at home." If I must say it myself, I can hold a pretty steady glass. My thing is wine. Dad frowned on that. "Boy, I don't want to be related to a wino. Grab a shot of straight bourbon or a cold beer. Better yet a shot of both. What the old-timers called a boilermaker. Now that's a man's drink."

I tried to be his kind of man. I'm not. Early on I remember wanting to tell him, "Look at me. I'm the kind of guy who digs other guys." I took off from home after that super-big beating. How could I stay tied to him when he hates me because of what I am. That from somebody who gave me life, a blood relative. My father spilled mine. My mother was hurt but she's used to hurting. She knows why I had to go. She looked like she understood.

This apartment, my apartment, I've made it a home. Nothing hardware or blue collar about it. I try for class. The rich look is also for poor folk. Some of my best furniture was found for free. I stripped paint and gussied up other folks' discards. A two-inch carved mahogany door turned into my coffee table. The trick: I call up city garbage disposal and ask what day they pick up large furniture items in some ritzy glitzy neighborhood. They might say Thursday and give the time. Well, I got out and combed the area before they arrived. Some days all I found was junk, others, pure treasure.

Jon landed on my doorstep in answer to a split-the-rent ad. He looked like class. Hell, he is class. But high-class acts often have a rotten board underneath the foundation. Whatever, rich or poor—and Jon's poor—class is class. Certain people are to the manner born. He's got it. We made a perfect team.

However, he lied to me about going home to see his parents two weekends. Both times there was a reason why I couldn't go along. A family problem needed to be ironed out and some other lame excuse. His mother scribbles postcards. He picks them up at his aunt's house and brings them home. I read them. Several times she mentioned a girl named Fern. "Fern sends her love. Can't wait to see you." So he was playing at having a girl to keep Ma and Pa happily in the dark. Receiving mail at his aunt's house! His parents didn't even know he lived with me. Guess he was afraid of getting static feedback. He was denying my existence. When someone is ashamed of the closest person in his life, the one he claims to prefer above all others, what does that say? He was determined to remain in the good graces of those who would condemn him.

Now he's writing from Minitown about books he left here and gave his forwarding address where to send them. That's a cry for help if ever I heard one. I bet he looked up Mini High in my schedule book, because I do have a commitment for an educational film showing at Minitown High. He's pulling a petty rip-off. Mini High is *my* contact, out of *my* schedule book. Next thing I hear, he's up there working. Come on. I shipped him his few books with no message enclosed. I also wrote to Mini High for my appointment with administration. It's best to take care of business before he bad-mouths me and ruins the deal.

I traveled up there in my interest, not his. Learned a lot and also got bashed in the face for the second time in my life. I could have had Barnett arrested. However, I did play a part in him having his butt about to be caught in a Minitown bear trap. Maybe I owe him something. We do happen to be—well let's call it brothers under the skin, or in the closet—mostly. Well, I feel sorry for him, that's all. Maybe I do miss him. I don't know why. What's to miss?

11 *Jonathan Barnett*

THE PHONE RANG THREE TIMES IN A ROW. THE same muffled voice gave the same nasty message. "Your faggot name is going to be all over the *Minitown Press.* That'll be a big help to Theodora Lynn's case. Witnesses—a faggot and his black student lover." I hung up, then took the receiver off the hook so I could think of something else. Like my second day of teaching at Mini High.

"A penny for your thoughts, teach," Rex Hardy's deep voice boomed at me. According to my work plan I'd give the students time to relax and look through brochures and manuals on their desks—time to unwind. As they chatted, my mind had gone back to Harp. Rex Hardy's voice brought me to attention. The scattering of students slumped into various poses, halfway, casually interested. Hardy, auditing, acted like he was generously hanging around to give me a helping hand.

The day before, some of them had put me through another test. A few class members had dropped out as a protest against me replacing Hardy. A dumb move. They dropped out while he sat in. Anyway, the course is not required. Students sure like to needle a new instructor. A young one like me really gets the in-depth treatment. Hardy is in charge of phys ed, which, in his case, means doing some of everything. Gym, swimming, baseball, track, basketball, volley ball, and mostly minding other people's business. Anything that comes up, he's likely to be in it.

He's about my height. Kind of heavy but moves fast. His hair is darkish brown and beginning to thin at the temples. He has a habit of smoothing both spots with both hands, wearing himself down, okay? He's one eager beaver, always turning in a busy performance. At the first session he had introduced me after making a long speech on his "fruitful efforts" to bring computers to Mini High and ending with, "I've heard that our talented new instructor, Mr. Jonathan Barnett, may soon have us processing funds out of banks, or tuning in on FBI files. Of course that's a joke, but we have heard of kid hackers good enough to pull off a few illegal tricks. I'm more interested in mathematical applications. However, Principal Mitchell has wisely placed emphasis on starting with word processing." Long-winded guy. He kept me on hold and shifted into discussing video games, ignoring me for almost ten minutes. At last he slowed down and gave me the go sign to interrupt. I wouldn't. He rattled on, then slowed again. Finally he quit. I started off trying to imitate my dad's easygoing teaching style.

"Each of you has a far better computer than any on the

market today. I'm talking about your brain. It holds all your years of information, and it's busy storing more every second. Whatever you're thinking or planning, your brain is saving it, adding up the score. Now the cold hardware machines we have here carry programs prepared by somebody to make our planned work go faster and easier."

I was lost for a minute. Didn't know where the next word was coming from. My mind went blank. Theodora Lynn raised her hand, her lovely saving hand.

"Mr. Barnett, what is word processing?"

A few giggly girls called out, "Oh, Theo, do your thing."

The students wore name tags for the first lesson. My dumb idea. That had also drawn snickers. Theodora had pasted her name over her left tit. Her clinging tee shirt announced in green sparkling letters, "It's all here." She is one well-rounded girl. She had puckered her lips to prettily pronounce processing. Next she unpinned her ponytail. A fountain of blond waves fell around her shoulders. She threw her head back and shook her hair forward, back again and then from side to side. Her golden mane was on the way to lighting up the room, but I sure wished she wouldn't finger comb her tresses with such abandon. A fine mist of dry hairspray or maybe it could have been dandruff showed up as a halo of dust. Susan Tate, one of our two black students, made a quiet to-do of fanning and pressing a tissue to her nose, as if fighting off suffocation. I tried to get in control of my lesson.

"Miss Lynn, will you write a sentence on the blackboard? Any sentence."

She strolled up and printed, "Welcome to Mini High."

"Now change it in some way," I said.

She added on, "Mr. Barnett." "Well, yes, that's a change," I said, as she slowly drifted back to her seat. "That is word processing. Miss Lynn has written and edited a sentence. Er—we may process words by using pencil on paper, chalk on a blackboard, writing with crayons on a brown paper bag, or by typing."

One of the giggling girls stopped long enough to say, "Or try using a ballpoint pen."

Miss Lynn smiled and sweetly said, "Drop dead, fan club member."

I tried to ignore the horseplay. "We are going to go through the process of arranging and rearranging words on a computer." I was wishing class was over. Forty-five minutes can feel like forever. Who needs to be laughed at while they are trying to teach? All of a sudden there was a rat-a-tat sound—another and another. It was Rex Hardy tapping his foot. He was wearing brown leather sports shoes with metal tips on the heels and toes. He stopped clattering and explained, "I wear metal caps to keep from turning them over—and also to warn evildoers that I'm approaching. Most of the time I'm in running shoes in case I have to get away in a hurry." He got a laugh, then went back to tapping again. Hardy was deliberately trying to keep me from teaching. Straight on was the only way to go.

I turned to Tyrone Tate, Susan's brother. "This is a floppy disk. Our word-processing program is recorded on it. Why do you think it's called a floppy disk?"

"Because it's floppy, like, flexible?"

A kid wearing the Spencer Reese name tag had a crewcut that looked like it was clipped by a dull lawn mower. His mouth held to one expression, a smirk. He gave out a fresh remark. "Hey, that's right-on brilliant. Let's appoint Tyrone Tate to sit on the Supreme Court, why don't we?" He waved a long thin arm in my direction and casually added, "*Mr.* Barnett, why not tell us why the machine is named a computer. Please tell, huh, why don't you, sir?"

He needed a fast knuckle job across his lip, but that's not part of the course. "Why are you called Spencer Reese?" I asked.

"That's what my folks named me, sir."

"Same answer goes for the hardware. The original manufacturers get to name whatever lousy product they create."

I got my first good laugh on that. The black girl, Susan Tate, had started it off. She's got to be the neatest dresser in town. Real trendy. Light sweater, skirt and shoes, shiny braided blue-black hair. Lots of braids—like an Egyptian painting. She pays strict attention, takes notes. Tyrone Tate and Theodora Lynn have turned out to be the most promising students. Theo has a slight edge, really. Forgets nothing. She doesn't know how smart she is. Seems to feel stupid. Always trying to mark herself a fool before someone beats her to it. She hung around after the others left. Asked permission to take a manual home. I found the courage to say, "Settle down now, Theodora. Don't be afraid." Before long she eased up on public preening, stopped flinging her hair in everyone's face and stirring it up with her fingers.

At each session I noticed Rex Hardy's eyes following her every move. He seemed to feel more than a teacher ought to feel about a student. Whenever she gave a correct answer Hardy reached out to pat her knee. She'd give him a stern look, then he'd withdraw his hand and softly drum the floor with those silly metal taps. Spencer Reese spent too much time coldly staring at the two blacks, Susan and Tyrone. Meanly staring. He caught me watching him once or twice, and turned on that smirk.

Teaching is not for me. It was a daily struggle to gain a little respect and keep some discipline and find out how best to pass on information. Teaching takes too much damn thought. At home, even before you get to school, you have to prepare the lesson. And then there are those endless papers—progress reports—to write up, papers to take home, papers and more papers.

One afternoon when class was over Rex Hardy almost complimented me. "Barnett, you're really coming along."

"Thank you, Mr. Hardy," I said and meant it. 'Cause my insides needed a little praise. I was fast finding out that really knowing a subject does not necessarily make a good teacher. That's not enough. You have to learn how to deal with all kinds of people, those under and over you. Well, maybe that comes with more experience.

In a day or two Rex Hardy acted confidential and told me he thought the missing students would soon return. I guess he meant they will show up whenever he gives the okay signal. No, knowing your subject is not enough. You have to learn how to *control* people and become a leader in the game of educational politics.

Back to Lataweeze here. Did you ever see a cat sleep on its back with paws up in the air? She thinks she's a person. The phone keeps me busy, rings whenever I put it back on the hook. The poison mouth again. "You faggot you." I hang up, pick up—and hang up again.

I think of running away, bus on back home. Knock on the door and ask my mother to make pancakes. What home? Home is not home anymore. Lataweeze turns over and sleepily watches me. She naps with one eye almost open. Rests one of 'em at a time. Maybe she can't trust to close both. She sure knows how to stretch her feet, relax her toes, fan out the sharp claws. She relaxes and they disappear into the fur. She yawns and shows pearly sharp little teeth. Lataweeze, be glad you're not a teenager who's a gay, inexperienced computer instructor. Rejoice in your catness. Be glad to be what you are.

Funny, I thought of taking my life more than once. Well, not so funny. Doesn't make sense. And yet it does. But only if you let it. The hardest thing to go on is feeling that nobody likes who and what you are. Yeah, that has something to do with why Theodora flings her hair around. And why Spencer Reese stares, why Rex Hardy interrupts my teaching, why Tyrone Tate stares out of the window. And why, and why, and why. It's all about who we are, and how unpleasing that may be—to other people.

12 Theodora Lynn

I SHOULD CHARGE REX HARDY WITH MORE THAN attempted rape. It ought to be attempted murder. Holding his rough hand over my mouth to keep me from screaming. I was choking. My father has a lawyer on my case. We'll soon see some punishment handed out because of what happened.

There's a crumby trick that goes on at Mini High. A mean, fun way to see if you're a good sport. They hem you in somewhere and give you the business. You might get your butt locked in a classroom or in the basement—anywhere. Our compu-class is on upper basement level. Mrs. Mitchell needed a few extra rooms for smaller classes. Board of ed built study spaces. Cubbyholes, really. Upper basement has a long hall, doors on each side open onto study spaces, little classrooms. In-the-know, long-term teachers seldom use them. Who wants to teach boxed in upper basement? Gym is at the end of the hall. Swimming pool's behind that. Upper basement is the pits. Dreary. A lot of hanging out goes on down there when gym and pool are not being used. It's easy for lovers and goofers and illegal smokers to find an empty room and do their thing.

Basement schedule is always posted on main-floor bulletins. Anybody can tell if the coast is clear down below. At least they could before Barnett came and really used the place.

Principal Mitchell gave him one of the cubbyholes for his class. That's almost like having a security man on the floor. Somebody thought he might be a spy. They had read about how the police department once sent in young cops who posed as students, but they were drug-busters. Anyway, that was another school. The cleaning closet is near the gym. It's used to store mops, pails, brooms, disinfectant and stuff. That door has a heavy slide bolt on the *outside.* If you go in there somebody could slam it and lock you in. There's no light and no window. A disinfectant dungeon.

One time they locked in Tony-Marie. Some boy was waiting for her. He rubbed her boobs. She almost went berserk and had a good time making a fuss about it, for weeks. But she never reported a name. Pretended she couldn't see in the dark. You can bet she knew. Loved being the center of attention. Word began to go around that someone was going to pull a trick on Jonathan Barnett. That's no fair. He's a teacher. Anyway an instructor. They just wanted to pick on him because he's smart. They hate having a smart young guy telling them what to do.

Spencer Reese had started a rumor that Barnett's gay.

Dull people sure love to make up cheap, tacky excitement. I tried to warn Barnett. We were passing each other in the hallway and I said, "Look out, don't go in the closet." He gave me the strangest sad kind of look and said, "Let's watch what we *say*, Theodora." Seems like I can't do anything right. However.

I was remembering how he once told me, "Don't be afraid, Theodora." Oh, well, you can't win even when trying to protect a person. But he has done things for me. Gave me poise. I hated to stand by and let an ignoramus like Spencer Reese run a lie on a decent person. I know how it feels to be picked on. Spencer wants parents to think how kids aren't safe around funny-sexed people. I know more about that than he does. But he was setting up Barnett, scaring people by saying the guy might have AIDS, just because he's kinda skinny. Well I took care of that with a fearless rebuttal. Everybody I met got the same message. "Jonathan Barnett is not *gay* and he does not have *AIDS*." I passed that out on handwritten cards. A dumb gal named Shelly asked, "How do you know what he is or isn't, or what he has or has not? Is it by rumor or firsthand, direct experience?" I told her that I met him before he ever got to Minitown and I happen to know he's madly in love with a beautiful girl named Fern—who lives near his parents in Marsley Falls.

Dad's gone off to see about the lawyer without me, but at least he's doing it. The house next door, Tyrone's, is shut tight, with shades down. That means I'm not to come over. All this crap, just as I was beginning to feel glad about myself.

I had been so sad all the time I didn't realize how great

it could feel to be happy. I'd never been good at studies before. It was really fine to be running ahead of the pack in compu-class and also in *math.* Who knows, maybe someday I could be ahead of everybody in every subject. Only thing wrong with compu-class is Rex Hardy and Spencer Reese. Hardy hates competition. Spence is worked up over blacks in class, in school, in the world, really. I wish my father had never gone to Spencer's dumb dad to get up a petition for the Tates to move. He said that Spencer Reese said, "Mr. Lynn, who's going to move just because you ask them to do it?" He puts his mean mouth right in the middle of everything older people do. Takes charge.

I was so glad to be great in compu-class. I got a feeling of power from knowing that there was one thing I knew better than any of the others. Solid, surely, knew it.

One morning last week after a quick orange juice, on my way flying out of the house, Mom stopped me. "Why you look absolutely beautiful, Theo."

"I do? Well, thanks."

"I'm glad you didn't put your face on today."

I looked in the wall mirror. "Gee, Mom, I forgot to do my makeup. I'm in a hurry to learn a couple of new formats before compu-class. Barnett lets me set up the machine early." I grabbed a lipstick from my denim shoulder bag. Gave a couple of quick swipes and mummed my lips together.

"Oh, Theo, you look just fine without it," she said.

"Well, Mom, no need to send Mini High into shock over any sudden changes."

My mother looked like she felt proud of me. "I'm glad

you're doing well in something, Theo," she said. "You're showing so much progress. Maybe it all depends on who's the teacher."

"Yeah," I said. "But also I can trust a machine. It treats everybody the same way. And that also goes for mathematics, for numbers. A machine and numbers. They both have to be as fair to one person as to another."

I started to put my arms around my mother. I didn't. We don't do that kind of stuff. Anyway whenever I get too close to anyone it makes me remember Uncle Ed and that touching. Closeness makes me nervous. The head shrinker and our minister, everybody says, "Don't look back, Theo." They like to say that. Where else shall I look?

"Mom, you think Dad might buy me a computer? It would help with my other subjects."

"That's an expensive item, Theo," she said.

"Yeah, but the Tates have one. I went over there and used theirs." Just then Mom looked out of the window. Tyrone and his standoffish sister, Susan, were leaving for school. He was dressed real neat and she looked, as always, like a magazine model advertising teenage clothes. "Gee, Mom," I said, "they have everything."

"Theo, some people, including some coloreds, have more than we do. Why fret about it?"

"I'm not jealous of what anybody else has, Mom. I just want more things for myself."

She stopped me from leaving. "Wait. Hold on, honey. Don't go yet. Let them walk ahead. Take the other way around to school. Your father does not want you getting too close. And stay out of that house. Learn to be friendly and cordial while keeping your distance."

"Oh, Mom, I can't duck them every day. They live right next door. And Barnett did make Tyrone my compu-partner. We have to work together."

She stopped loading the washing machine. "Theo, why the devil did he do that? Why in the hell? He must be crazy!" Oh, she can unleash her temper too.

"Mom, we're working in teams. One helps the other. Like I might remember what my partner forgets, or the other way around. Teaming up just makes the work go easier. Everybody in class is teamed."

"Yes, but I don't think it showed sensitivity on the part of the teacher."

"Oh, come on, why?"

"To put a white girl with a black boy is not a thoughtful thing to do. Boy with boy would be more tactful."

"Tyrone and I are the ones doing the best work."

"Well, don't get too chummy. Keep your distance. Remember who you are."

"Who am I, Mother?"

"Oh, Theo, you know what I mean. You're white and that's—well, it's important. You can be polite and still keep your distance. We don't need any more negative talk. Stay away from the wrong kind of friends." The whole good feeling we had was gone.

The real trouble started when some dumb jokester slipped a sealed envelope under my locker door. There was a note inside. "Dear Hot Stuff, I wrote a juicy story about you and your Uncle Ed. Porny-corn! I hid your bedtime story somewhere. Find your secret, and it's all yours. Fail, and your butt's in trouble. Somebody else will get to read it. Follow the CLEWS." That mean note made me sick. Leaning against my cold locker door, I stole a glance up and down the hallway. I heard laughing down at one end. Someone might have been nearby, watching, studying how I was taking the message. I wasn't taking it too well. Nobody, but nobody, knew about Uncle Ed except Mom, Dad, my head shrinker, a medical doctor and Uncle Ed himself, who's now thousands of miles away. Shrinks, like med doctors, are not supposed to tell. Okay, how about Mom? No way would she tell that. What about Spencer Reese's dad? He's my dad's distant friend. Used to be his closest. Dad just might have once told him about it. However, if Spence Jr. ever heard it, I'm in trouble. My parents tell other people that I go off to visit a cousin when I'm being sent out of town for therapy. There's a therapist right here in Minitown, but they don't want that. Mom says secrets can't be kept that way. I'm finding out they can't be kept, period.

I leaned against the steel locker trying to work up the nerve to ignore the message. The last part gave directions. "Go to your computer. Call up B: HOTS MSS. on drive B." There was a disk on top of my computer. I turned on, inserted it in the machine and called it up. The machine flashed a message on the monitor. "Hi, Hot Stuff. Go to subbasement boiler room. West window, find disk."

Like, hypnotized, I headed for the subbasement. Just as I was about to open the door marked No Trespassing, Mrs. Kaplan, a super-nosy science teacher, was passing. She butted in. "Why are you going to the basement? That door should remain closed." I told her I had mistaken it for the ladies room. Dumb lie. I hurried away, then looked back. She was watching me. I ran back upstairs and waited a while. Soon it would be class time. Again I tried for subbasement. Made it. It was dark. Only exit and work lights on. Feeling my way along a wall I ran my fingers into a corner spider web. Yuck. Next, west window. Had to climb on a packing box to reach the sill. Yeah, there was an envelope, no disk inside. A note. "Excuse. Look east window." There are *two* east windows. I looked on the wrong ledge first while praying nobody from maintenance or security would come in and catch me at it. The disk was on the second windowsill. I handled it carefully, so's not to mess up the message, and went back upstairs to the exit door, hoping no one would see me sneaking out of the boiler room. I waited. One, two, three pairs of footsteps went by. Then silence. I opened the door. All clear. The new disk delivered. The message on the monitor read: "Sweetie. Secret about Ed is on top shelf of cleaning closet this floor. Finder keeper, loser weeper."

I started out, but in came Barnett, Tyrone and his sister, Susan. It had to wait. I don't trust anybody anymore. Susan was looking everywhere but at me, as usual. Spence showed up, grim jawed and cold eyed. They all seemed innocent. There was a lot of noise outside, laughing and shouting. "Mini High, High, High!"

Cheerleaders rehearsing for the public parade. I should have been out there. How dare Hardy hold rehearsals during Barnett's class time. I was ready and dressed for it, but I asked, "Mr. Barnett, did you know about cheerleader practice during this period?"

"No, I didn't, Theo." Then I asked Tyrone's sister, "Did you, Susan?"

"No, but, after all, I'm not a member of it." She looked at me as if it's my fault she isn't a member. Nobody ever asked me. I went to Hardy and *demanded* in. I turned out to be the leader of all leaders. Let present cheerleaders eat their jealous hearts for dinner.

I looked out of the window. They were practicing, but Hardy wasn't there. I asked to urgently leave the room and left before getting Barnett's permission. I went to that cruddy, dark closet to search. Reached the top shelf by standing on a shaky scrub pail. Nothing up there but dust and the smell of cigarette smoke. I kneeled on the floor and felt my way across the next row of shelves. I went behind a partition. A hot hand reached out and touched me as someone outside bolted the door—wham! slam! I almost jumped out of my skin. I knew it was Hardy, even in the dark. I started to scream. He put one hand over my mouth, the other hand grabbed my body. Felt like a hundred busy fingers. His mouth pressed against my ear. I felt warm breath and he was squeezing my breast. It hurt. I tried to get away. He twisted my arm. I couldn't move. He pulled me around to face him. Darkness couldn't hide who that was—Rex Hardy! I tried to scream. He closed his hand over my mouth. I could hardly breathe. He grabbed at my tee shirt, as I pulled away. It ripped.

"You keep it going, Theo. You ask for it!" He kept saying "You're the one who keeps it going, Theo. You ask for it." We both fell and hit the floor. Glass smashed in the dark. There was the smell of disinfectant. He kept tearing, pulling. I begged him, "Please, Uncle Ed, Mister Hardy, Uncle Ed, Mister Hardy—please, stop!" He wouldn't. I slammed my knee into his belly. He groaned. Suddenly the door opened. He let go and I flew out, screaming, holding my shirt together. I ran past Barnett, Tyrone and Spencer Reese.

Later I told about the disks. I told every single thing. But there were no notes or disks on, in or near my machine. Everything was gone. So the story is—I followed Hardy into that closet! I don't care what anybody thinks. Once, Uncle Ed made me feel ashamed. My mother and father were ashamed, too, because something terrible about sex happened to me. And now they are ashamed all over again. The school, the whole town must be talking. I cry off and on all day, like somebody died. Me, I'm the dead one. My parents won't let me go out. They did get a lawyer, but they didn't *want* to do it. Mom said, "This is the *second* time."

Dad said, "We're *sad* and very *disappointed.* But we're with you, Theo."

They're not acting mad. They're more like ashamed and hurt . . . forever. I'm stuck at home in prison.

Mini High's cheerleader section took part in the parade to unveil the founding father's memorial statue in the public park. Shelly took over my lead routine. Her picture was in our newspaper. She was even on local TV doing my steps. Where in the hell is justice? I'm trying not to be bitter . . . But honestly, there is such a thing as bitterness being right sometimes. You gotta have feelings.

13 *Susan Tate*

THEODORA LYNN'S NOTES AND DISKS WERE burning a hole in my purse. I buried the stuff in my dresser drawer. Then it started burning a hole in my mind. I thought about it every minute. It could be evidence of maybe a crime. Disks are only black squares with a hole in each middle and a notch on the side. But the crap's not mine and I had no right to steal . . . well, I didn't really steal. I simply carried the things home. I was afraid to take them back until I knew what was on them. Suppose there was something about my brother? Something awful? There's a big to-do since Theodora claimed important secrets are missing. Like proof that she was abused and assaulted. She's a nuisance! Gosh, who wants to be around a person who says she's been molested? A very respectable, studious boy in my English lit class, well, he said that Spencer Reese told him that Theo's father told his father that Theo was once sexually molested by a close relative. She seems to have a history of being in sex situations. This town is a number ten earthquake. A seven anyway.

My brother, Tyrone, and Theo were getting too computer friendly. She was even pushing herself into forbidden time in our basement to use our computer hands-on with my brother. Tyrone is too simpleminded. He likes everybody, even his enemies. His face lights up when that dumb Theo's on the scene. Once she sneaked over when her parents went downtown to buy a microwave oven. I sounded on Ty. "Here comes your number-one fan. She sure knows how to visit."

Tyrone shrugged me off. "Sue, I didn't send for her."

Maybe he didn't, but she walks in like *invited* and *welcome*. Me, I'd like to be back in Brooklyn where everybody acts normal. The two of them love to work the hell out of a computer and they understand all the stuff that I can't. They make me sick. The only kind of A-OK, friendly person in Mini High is Jonathan Barnett. So maybe he's too young to be teaching. He is too lax on discipline. It's tough for an instructor to be only a few years older than his students. Spencer Reese and old Rex Hardy give it to him, but mean. They walk all over him. He doesn't exactly let them. But they stay on his case. Me, I try to show respect, so I'm the one who gets the least attention. If you just go along and quietly do well, who wants to pay you any mind? Uncle Kwame says, "The wheel that does the squeakin' is the wheel that gets the grease." Make big noise if you want a little attention. Too many of these upper-middle-class brats squeak so much they have to go in for heavy therapy. They boast about it. "I'm in therapy." Well, hooray and la-de-da. They think having their empty heads examined is status. They boast about it 'cause it's expensive.

Dad told me, "You'd better learn to handle this Minitown flak because we can't move anywhere else except to the poor house or the cemetery—and both are overcrowded." These days all his sarcasm is laid on me because I won't conform to his mainstream methods.

On the big action day, I was in school at the computer, taking care of business. One minute everybody was around and then it turned into fast-exit time. Hardy had been marching in and sending cheerleaders outdoors to go through hectic practice routines on the gym bars. He told everybody that Principal Mitchell had given permission. Of course, Mitchell had not bothered to tell Barnett. Some of the kids were running in to play at computing or looking over my shoulder. All were wearing skimpy workout clothes except the few of us not in on cheering. They all started wandering around on their own, even going up on main floor to use the Coke machine. Theodora stood up, hopping from one foot to the other. "Mr. Barnett, may I leave the room. I have, have, have to go." Then she went. She loves to act like she's about to wet herself. Three other kids were outdoors standing on their heads. Not cheer-rehearsing or even thinking about computers. Hardy was in and out, taking over. He took charge. Busy making confusion. He was acting kinda angry. Said, "Where's the new hotshot Miss Choreographer? Is she still absent? Where's Barnett? I seem to be replacing all of my replacements." Then he was off and gone. Barnett had walked out of the room and into the gym. I heard a ball bouncing against the wall. I don't blame him, but a teacher is not supposed to go play handball during class time.

Ty, without a word to me, had joined Jonathan Barnett in the gym. Since everybody was doing whatever they pleased, I got up and went to the bathroom. There was nobody in authority to give permission anyway. Spencer Reese was still hanging around, but *alone* with him feels uncomfortable.

In the lav I washed my hands with that stinky liquid green soap. Refreshed my lipstick. Combed and fluffed out the ends of my front braids, then sat down at the makeup counter to read my new paperback, *Black and Madly in Love.* Why not? Everyone else was taking a vacation. Anyway, I can't read it at home in peace unless I'm locked in my room. In a few minutes Theodora crashed through the door like going for a touchdown. Her tee shirt was ripped open down one side, or else she had burst out of it. And no panties were to be seen under her torn shorts. She shoved past me and locked herself in one of the johns. "He tried to rape me! He tried to rape me!" She kept screaming. There are tiled walls in the lav, so the echo repeated, rape, rape, rape. I was scared but became the Red Cross and tried to be helpful. I asked her if I should call somebody. She paid me no mind. Just went on yelling and crying. "He's going to pay. You'll see. It's time for payday."

Suddenly I wondered if Theo was into starting up a race thing like her dad. If people burn crosses on your lawn you don't trust them about anything. My nerves were not ready for screams. Theodora's not my favorite person anyway. But only one question popped into my head, was she setting up my brother? Tyrone can be a pain in the neck, but he's almost too nice to people. Dad teases him about being overly kind. "Boy, you're so gentle, I bet you still believe in the Easter Bunny." Hardly. Ty has okay manners and he's patient and all that, but I've seen him fight toe to toe with boys bigger than himself. If anybody tries to harm anyone related to me I'll put a hurting on them that will make newspaper headlines for a month.

Okay, I left Theo in the john. I ran out in the hall. Ty, Barnett and that Reese boy and Hardy were standing in front of the cleaning closet. Barnett's face had turned dark red and sneaky snot-nosed Spence was grinning. Looking pleased. I was ready to help my brother fight if one of them jumped him. "Tyrone didn't hurt anybody," I said.

Barnett suddenly ran down the hallway, heading upstairs for main floor. Hardy, straightening his clothes, strolled to the men's room. Spence leaned against the closet door, looking mean. "Everybody clear out while you can."

"I'm not afraid of you, Spencer Reese," I yelled.

"Stay out of it, Susan!"

Tyrone grabbed my hand and pulled me into the classroom. I remember him saying, "Hardy did something to Theo."

"Take me home, Ty," I said. "I want to be home."

"We can't, Susan. School's still in session."

"Okay, well then I'm going home alone, all by myself."

He said, "I'll go with you after I check out the hall." He walked to the door and looked out.

Something caught my eye. On top of Theodora's machine were two disks in envelopes and two pieces of paper. I picked them up and slipped 'em in my purse, but fast. Something in the back of my mind told me to do it. Until that second I had never stolen—I mean *taken*—anything in my life. Tyrone came back. "The coast is clear." He put his arm around me. "Okay, Susan, let's go home."

"Are you in any trouble, Ty?" I asked.

"No, I hope not."

All of last weekend was a nightmare. Police went next door to the Lynns'. They also came to question Ty, but Dad said his children would not talk to them about anything without the advice of an attorney.

Tyrone told the family all he had seen. My parents and Uncle Kwame definitely did not want either of us involved in any testimony stuff as witnesses for or against Theodora or Mr. Hardy. Theodora's lawyer telephoned and Mom told him the same thing. "Unless they're summoned to court as witnesses our children will not volunteer information. They are *children*."

I began to feel better until Principal Mitchell phoned and asked my father, "Did Tyrone or Susan remove two floppy disks and any notes from the computer room?"

Dad asked us and we both said no. Mrs. Mitchell told him Theodora Lynn claims the material is important evidence. She asked us to immediately let them know if it turns up. I felt uncomfortable but angry about what was asked. First thing on somebody's mind is, "Did the *black* kids take something?"

We all quietly watched next door's comings and

goings. But there was no sign of Theodora. Mom said the grocery clerk told her that someone had told him how the girl had been delinquent in the past. Once she ran off to New York and stayed in a bus station all night—so maybe she did it again. I wondered how the clerk knew so much. Mom said, "Sue, every friend has a friend. That's how news travels. After all, if you can't keep a secret, what makes you think a friend can do it?" That sealed my lips even tighter about the stuff I took. But I was dying on the inside.

I know Theo Lynn is holed up in her own house and not in a bus station. One night I heard her crying. I got out of bed and walked in on Bubba doing math homework. He turns into Bubba when I need him real bad, Tyrone when he's tiresome and Ty when things are not too much one way or another. "Bubba, I hate to say this, but I have that missing disk material. I took it. I thought maybe something on it might hurt you, and I wouldn't want that."

"Gee, thanks, Sis."

"I don't like how her folks treat us. I can't find any good reason to care about helping Theodora. But I have the things they're looking for. Bubba, what shall I do?"

Whenever he hears "Bubba" he really comes to the rescue. But one time I called him that when trying to beg him out of his last peanut bar. He said "Knock it off, you phony." He knows when I'm for real.

"Did you read it?"

"I can't figure the code."

Down in the playroom we went to work. He took a

disk from the envelopes and shoved it in with his edit disk. He tried calling up her name, the name of the town and the family name. Nothing showed but blank new files.

"Ty, can't we just turn it in?"

"Susie, we may as well know what we're turning over."

He kept trying.

"Hey, dummy, you've been calling for the right information on the wrong disk. Answer one is on disk two and vicey-versey, okay?" We got the messages. Found out how she'd been frightened into the basement, then finally into the closet where Hardy must have been lurking in the dark. Ty made disk copies and note printouts. One of each to turn in, the rest as our backups in case someone decides to destroy our turned over evidence.

"Now who gets the original, Ty? Her parents? Her lawyer? The principal? The police? Or Theo herself?"

He sighed. "Sissy, it's show-and-tell time, and charity better begin here at home." Mom thought her parents should have the material. Dad opted for Mrs. Mitchell. We thought Uncle Kwame, who's courtwise, would say to go to the Lynns' attorney. I was surprised that he was not for handing in any evidence at all. He's got a grudge against Sam Lynn because he believes he was in on the cross burning. My father's just as certain that Lynn didn't do it. "Tell me this," he said, "would a man try to burn down a house next to his own? No way. Their lives and property could go up in flames along with ours. They were also asleep when the firemen arrived. Then too he did come over here and declare he had nothing to do with it. I can see the man is aging by the minute."

Uncle Kwame shook his head. "You taking up for that cracker? Max, you sound like the two of you might be having dinner together soon. Also, why did Barnett, the schoolteacher, drop over here one day to check out Ty's computer? Schoolteachers don't call on students anymore. Also, why does the white girl from next door pop in when you're away working? Next thing these mean townfolk will be calling Ty a queer, a rapist or both."

He had pinched my father's nerves. "You want us to move back to Brooklyn? I can't afford to do it!"

Uncle Kwame disagreed. "No way I want to see you run while somebody's trying to chase you. That's the time to stand pat and dig in. I'll be here until the air clears, although I don't like commuting back and forth on strange ground. However, if I go I'd be worrying myself to death back home. Just hanging around is boring, so let's make a move, okay? I'll hand Susie's loot over to that computer teacher."

Mom didn't like the idea. "He's hardly more than a child himself. It should be given to a responsible older person."

Uncle Kwame said, "No, they gave him the job and put him in charge of their computers and students, so let him see to all of it. I wouldn't give a damn if he wasn't but five years old. Give the responsibility to the one they made responsible."

Dad started dealing cards, laying out a hand of solitaire for himself. That's what he does when he gets tired of us. Uncle Kwame said, "Don't be so selfish, brother. Let's play poker, five card draw, red aces and black tens wild."

My father went on with his game. "No, I'll just flip solitaire cards and study my own thoughts. By the way, I have an interview this evening about becoming a member of the country club. I'll be the first one of *us*."

Uncle Kwame laughed like crazy, stamped his feet the way he likes to do when he's extra tickled. "Brother, you are accepted. The town press put you and that fire right over the top. That article about someone burning a cross on your lawn, and this being the town's only black family, oh, that was a real tearjerker. You might get popular enough to become their first African-American mayor."

My mother smiled kind of sickly. "I hope none of our friends back in Brooklyn saw the local television coverage. Sounded like our main goal in life is to live with whites. However, just like winning a 50-million-dollar lottery, some secrets are hard to keep. We do live surrounded by white neighbors."

Dad gave up on his card game. "Kwame, why did you offer to take the disk material to Barnett? You don't think I can speak for my family? Do you really take me for a coward?"

"No, but you have enough to do to watch your kids, your wife and your lawn. I care about all of you, okay? But I didn't come up here to chat foolishness. I came to lay my life down if need be. You have never ever wanted any favors, not from anybody. And certainly not from me. You're about bootstrapping it all the way, all by yourself. But if you can accept those white club boys taking you in on their golf green, you can accept your black brother speaking on behalf of your children. I want to *do* something for you now because when I go you'll still be here holding down the fort. I'm offering my services. Yes or no, it's up to you."

Dad started picking up cards, stacking them up, building a card house. He does that real fine, without a wobble. Finally he said, "Brother, will you kindly deliver the disk to the computer teacher? I would appreciate that very much."

We all smiled and were glad he had said it. Mom had the last word. "Susan, after this keep your hands off of other people's property." She won't have to tell me twice.

Dad suddenly changed his mind. "Kwame, you and I, let's go to the principal first. Start at the top."

14 *Spencer Reese*

MY FATHER USED TO SAY HOW HE WOULD LIKE me to some day be the founder and first president of a new organization called The National Association for the Advancement of White Power. Now he's down to promising me a computer if I just pass Compu-One. He's also kinda sore because I won't study the guitar Gramps gave me last Christmas. I don't want a guitar or a computer. I want a motorcycle. Dad's okay, more of a white man than most you'll find in Minitown. He used to be.

He and his buddies cool off and lose nerve as they get older. They still meet once in a while. But they can't move it anymore. They seem to think you can bad-*mouth* an enemy to death. Nothing's that easy. Sam Lynn, Theodora's dumb dad, used to come around and talk nonstop. Then he cut his visits to once in a while. He came running back when the dinge family moved next door to him. My father called a meeting and gathered a flock of chickens. They talked about getting up a petition to ease out undesirables. Sam Lynn, after starting the noise, changed his mind, backed out and now doesn't even want his name on the petition paper because, "It's hard to frame an exact charge. We can't just put down that they're coloreds. Sounds too racist. Couldn't a group get together and offer to buy them out? Then, after they're gone, we can resell."

Tom Jennings, my father's best friend, nixed that. "They won't do it. Why should anybody be willing to sell out of a place they just bought?"

One old guy gave them a small laugh. "If I lived next door to Sam Lynn maybe I'd be glad to move."

Sure, they laughed over that. But Tom Jennings scored again. "They have to *know* they're unwanted. Then maybe they'll be glad to be bought out."

After that they hassled around in a pass-the-buck kind of way. Thought up more mild stuff, like the cold-shoulder shutout. One old guy reminded them of when the first Jew family moved here. Some businessmen put the silent squeeze play on them, didn't deliver their heating oil during a bad cold snap. The way the game works is, like, oil company plays dumb and says they sent the oil. They promise to look into the matter. Then comes the stall-and-wait action. Enough low service or no service from businesses can bug some people enough to get the message and move the hell on out. It doesn't work with everybody. Jews are now all over the place. According to my father it's because they know how to hire lawyers, hassle the mayor, and even get to the governor. My father also says they're more united than we are. Even though some are atheists.

Darkies are also united. They can hang in there. Sam Lynn is shaky because his sexy daughter, Theo—I call her "Hots"—is loose as a goose on castor oil. She sure knows how to show it all off. She's got a thousand ways of asking for rape. At school Theo throws one leg over her desk, playing cool while making guys sweat. She wears tight pants, or skirts so short you can see eternity. Just as I'm getting off on the view she pulls herself together and sits like a saint.

Jonathan Barnett invited me to join study-period chess games with Tyrone and Susan Tate. That was his sneaky way of bringing about better race relations, which seems to be a big deal with him. I said okay and then didn't show up. Hots has to make out-of-town trips to a shrink to get her eggs unscrambled, all because she diddled around with her Uncle Ed, Sam Lynn's brother. Lynn swore my father to keep that a secret. Dad didn't tell another soul—except the guys who hang out here. One of the old boys told us something. "That new kid Jonathan Barnett's nothing but a fruit on the prowl, according to Rex Hardy."

Well, Theodora's in a first-class mess now. I computerized her into that cleaning closet. My father said her father had better hurry and protest his new neighbors out of town before he becomes grandpa to a mulatto baby.

The dark intruders have a son named Tyrone and an uppity daughter named Susan. They are not at all humble on white turf. They also like to show off their Cadillac and wear ritzy clothes. Tate Sr. has put in an application to join the country club. Word's out that he's going to be accepted. How about that? White guys voting a dinge in and turning down some of their own. Mrs. Mitchell, our bleeding-heart principal, personally invited the Tate woman to join parent-teacher. Some stupid woman baked a cake with the word welcome in icing for her very first meeting. Did any white woman ever get a welcome cake? My mom didn't. She doesn't like to go anyway.

My father says he's disgusted with backward white people. Fine, but what's his crowd doing about it? A bunch of supposed-to-be-tough guys, just sitting around shaking their heads and grumbling. Talk without action.

Jonathan Barnett, the kid compu-wonder, fusses over the dinges like they're God's gift to the nation. My father and his crowd better forget the chill-out treatment. The Tates don't care if we never speak to them. They just go right on buying stuff, getting invited into other people's country clubs, and having cakes baked for them.

Me and my friend Billy, we sit there listening to the old guys, our parents, shoot the breeze. They get us so worked up, we can hardly sit still. Then the heat dies down and they "table" the action. "Let's monitor the situation."

Jonathan Barnett, I bet he is a genuine, for real swish. The kind who doesn't care what color he's swishin' with. We don't need that here, okay? Some say Mister Trevers, my science teacher, is also kind of queer. But at least he walks, talks and acts manly, so it's hard to nail the charge down. He is a loner. Old enough, but still not married and no girlfriend. They better monitor his situation. My father says never trust people who look or act too different from everybody else.

At the last gathering of the old buddies, Dad said they have to wait for justice until whites and blacks finally square off on each side of a battlefield and shoot it out. I wonder when's that to be. My friend Billy and I—we decided to show the old guard how things can still get done. I'd like to live all the way back to the days of the Wild West with Jesse James or Daniel Boone. They didn't sit around monitoring situations. Move was the name of their game. That's what counts. Why should an outside fruit's word be taken as truth against inside normal guys?

That Jonathan got the bright idea of teaming up pairs of compu-partners. He asked me to work with the dark invader, Tyrone. Privately I stood up for my civil rights like they do. "No thanks, I want a white partner if it's all the same to you. And even if it's not all the same."

"I don't understand," he said.

"Well," I asked, "would you like to have my dad come to school and explain it for you?"

"No thanks, Spencer, I'll figure it out on my own."

Rex Hardy explained to me how come Barnett wasn't interested in joining our weekend jogout. He said, "Spence, all guys are not like us. Not on the macho side." He gave a big wink to put across his message.

Jonathan teamed Theo with Tyrone Tate. Did she back off? Hell no. While her father was busy trying to clean out the unwanted, his daughter teams up with them. That's sick. Barnett has her hypnotized. She could not get along with anybody. Now she's working with blacks. The queer pushed her into being partners with Ty. I bet he's trying to hide that maybe he's the one who digs him. Hots would jump off the roof if Barnett asked her to do it. Well, now she's in the pits. Out to do in Hardy with the help of a dinge and a queer. About what? A touch or a grab on a gal who used to make out with her uncle at age nine? According to her own father! Also, Tyrone, the black guy, has to have one eye out for getting a white girl . . . they all do.

A guy named Harper Mead came to town for just a week. Supposed to be drumming up something about showing a school film. Whenever Principal Mitchell gets an extra dime in the school budget she tries to "expand horizons." My mother said the only thing she sees expanding is Mitch's big butt. My father said that Rex Hardy told a clerk at Emporium Food Supply that the film guy used to be Barnett's lover in New York City. Wow. He also passed the news to Barnett's landlady, old Violet Trale, so she could keep an eye out for what goes on in her house. Trale told my mother, and asked her not to repeat the story. Too late, the whisper's out by phone. It may as well be flashed on the evening news.

Some people are pissed off by Theo yelling attempted rape over that silly closet bit. Getting locked in was just fun, even if she did get a touch on the tit. Lots of kids play jokes, and some get tricked. After all, be a sport. She didn't die or get hurt. Hardy may not be the most brilliant teacher at Mini High, but he is a good sport. *Attempted* rape, hell, people are *attempting* to get to Mars but nobody's done it yet, okay? Sure, I locked Theo and Hardy in the closet. Somebody needs to stir her porridge until it's well cooked. The best time to do it was busy Friday. The last period of the day when everybody was cheer practicing or goofing off somewhere. What I meant to do was send Hots in and then Hardy. I was putting him up to do it . . . but he wasn't even listening. He laughed me off, didn't even hear me. *Pure luck*. He just happened to go hide in there to steal a smoke. He may jog but he also sneaks smokes. He went in the right place at the right time. When she walked in wearing that flowery perfume—it set off his alarm clock. Hell, what's the big fuss about? There wasn't any letter about "Uncle Ed" anyway. That was just a joke. However . . . damned if I'm going to tell how I was the one who did it. Let every tub stand on its own bottom!

Only a few days before, my "Operation Dinge" went down. I thought up an MO—modus operandi—the original action. Action! That's what counts. I thought it up. Me and Billy, we moved in on Sam Lynn's lousy unwanted neighbors.

Billy overslept the week before but, the next week, we got synchronized and met on time, at three in the morning. We crept out of our houses, met up, and carried out our number one W.W.—Wild West—plan.

I had made a cross out of two metal rods wrapped in rags. Billy brought a bottle of kerosene to soak it. When we got there, every house on Lynn's block was pitch dark. We climbed over the enemy's back fence, then belly crawled our way to the front lawn. My heart was jumping in my throat as we leaned that cross against the house and set it on fire. Action is not easy, okay? I bet we were back in our beds before the fire engines arrived. I was out of breath from hopping fences, jumping a ditch and taking the long way home. But mission was accomplished.

Now Dad says Sam Lynn's headed to cracksville, denying he had anything to do with that next-door fire. Yeah, you ought to hear him. "Living next door, would I do a thing like that? Would I?"

Lynn used to be a pretty good guy. Well, whatever he was, he's now a chicken-heart coward. My father also says, "Somebody in this town has guts. And whoever he is, he made my day. I wonder who's the hero?" He guesses and guesses. If he knew, I bet he'd be proud of me. But I'll never tell him and Billy won't tell his folks either. We both know chickens are not to be trusted. Not even when they're blood relatives.

15 Jonathan Barnett

I WISH I COULD WISH MYSELF A THOUSAND miles away, somewhere far enough not to be the cause of trouble for anybody else. You can't even move out of town without somebody catching up with you.

A few days ago, I was minding my business and stumbled upon the unexpected. Staked out and waiting. I left school, making a fast exit for home before a student could corner me for overtime compu-talk. Well, there the hell he was, leaning tall against the school gate, wearing a sky-blue denim sports suit and an innocent smile. Harper Mead. I stopped to exchange greetings as if we were casual friends who seldom meet. "Well, Harper, what's new?"

"I didn't track you down, believe me. This is accidental."

I said, "Some accident. It really took you out of your way."

"I had business with your principal. Let's talk."

"About what?"

"It's kind of important."

I took him out of the way to a scroungy beer joint near the train depot. I was glad we had a dim, quiet booth and tired service from a waitress who looked like she'd rather be home. There were only a few customers around. All were quietly drinking beer.

"Jonathan," Harp said, "I'm here setting up appointments to show a film and lecture program. Remember *my idea* to tape all of the main colleges and campuses around the country, so high school kids will know more about where they'd like to go for college? It's sort of a courtesy project. Financed by Mack & Tower Textbooks. Jon, are you listening?"

"Yeah, sounds good."

"I'm setting up screenings for next semester at the invitation of a teacher, Mr. Hardy, and your principal. They answered my Mack & Tower inquiry."

"Oh, knock it off, Harp, and get down to it."

"Well, this guy Hardy took me to the Wayward Garden so I could lay out the project and date in a showing. He happened to drop your name and I mentioned that I knew you, that in fact once we lived together, I mean how we shared the New York apartment."

"Busy, aren't you? Your mouth should be declared a lethal weapon."

"Well, not to worry." The way he said it made me worry. He apologized for being too *honest* and *straightforward.*

"Thank you, Saint Harp. That halo pinches your head a little."

"Oh, come on. Forget the past Jon, shake hands."

I felt childish reaching over the paper-napkin holder to shake his outstretched hand. His right eye twitched. "You really don't care anymore about me do you, Jon?"

"I hope not."

"How do you turn off so easily?"

"Tell me, Harper, what happened to last year's snow?"

"It's gone, melted. I get it."

"Right. That's how I turn off. You wanted someone to own, Harp, a grateful slave. I was always humbling myself. Low man on the totem pole in exchange for your kindness and approval." I wouldn't give him a chance to break in. "You were a kind master, but I don't want to be owned. Whenever anybody asked me a question, damn if you didn't butt in and answer for me. Right in front of my eyes, you'd flip through my mail before handing it over."

"What mail? All that came to my place were circulars. Your personal mail went to your aunt's house, remember?"

"Harp, you were bossy. All that public confession about coming out. Your call to my parents. Doing my confessing for me. Man, you almost killed them. My only out was to walk away from you. I didn't want to go but I've done it. Now, good luck with your college project. Have a success."

"Jonathan, there's more I want to tell you. I have to tell you."

"Let go, Harp, I don't want to hear it."

He was hard to shake. Never gives up in a hurry. He walked beside me, tagging along. Even though I shook hands again and said good-bye as we left the bar. It's hard to hate him. I thought of our better days, reading aloud from good books, having lunch at the Museum of Modern Art. Outlining projects. And then he blurted it out.

"Jon, there's something else. Rex Hardy bought me one too many of the damned dry martinis and I let it drop. I told him about our relationship."

We were passing an empty lot. Suddenly I could hardly breathe. "You let what drop?"

Harp's face turned deep red. Head down, he spat out half-choked words, unable to look me in the face. "But if he ever repeats or tries to hurt you with anything I've said, I swear I'll call him a liar. Jon, I mentioned our relationship—just in passing."

I landed a punch in his face and he was lying at my feet, sprawled out on the edge of the lot, his body surrounded by old tin cans and trash. I stood ready, waiting for him to jump to his feet and pulverize me. He could have done it. I'm no match. I'm smaller and weaker. But I was mad enough to die on the defense. He sat up, rubbing his chin, and wiped away a trickle of blood. "Thanks, Jon-baby, for the great finish. Let's now call all scores even." I turned and walked away feeling lousy.

Even stretched out on the ground Harp was in charge of the situation. Why do I come out feeling wrong all the time? Even my students assert themselves more than I do. Other people, the black kids, Susan and Tyrone, they're strong. They meet things head-on. I run away to shut people out, but they won't allow me to do it. They never do. Dropping out is not allowed.

So now they're about forcing me to speak up in front of the school board in favor of Rex Hardy, the alleged attempted rapist. Who needs it? I don't like reporting myself or anybody else. Theodora's parents don't need it, and certainly not Hardy. Anonymous phone callers threaten to nail my ass in public. I feel extra sorry for Theodora Lynn. They're going to pitch poison darts at her too. Why? My landlady says, "Well, she did run away from home once. That doesn't look nice." So. I ran too, in my own way. But bloodhound people will hunt you down until they find you. Why am I being pushed to speak up *for* Rex Hardy? One answer, to make Theo look like a liar. They want to shoot her story down, mainly because she's not the most popular figure around, I guess. Those known as *anonymous* are secretly pushing hard to make someone, namely me, just *hint* that Theo could be a liar. To plant a little doubt, just enough to nix her story. Theo can be an exaggerating nuisance, but I don't believe she's a liar. A teacher attacked a student in a clean-up closet while they were both locked in. Two people in trouble. Maybe three. Who locked them in? Spencer Reese is my guess.

She screamed. I unbolted the door and she ran out of the dark, clothes torn. There was Rex Hardy, face turned toward the wall, head down like guys arrested on the nightly news. Theo took off down the corridor to the girls' lav.

Two people saw that scene. Me and Tyrone Tate. The next day Hardy was arrested. He got himself a lawyer and was bailed out in his own care in no time flat. An office clerk in the principal's office repeated what she'd heard from another repeater. "Everybody knows that girl Theodora is a sick liar." Well, I believe he did what she says he did.

I'm sorry I saw anything. I have enough to worry about. My father has been in and out of the hospital. It was two weeks before Mom told me. "We didn't want you to know until the worst was over. Tests showed it wasn't really a full heart attack, but he is definitely a heart patient." I wondered if the gay situation had worried my father into the hospital.

"Why didn't you tell me, Mother?"

"We didn't want you to worry."

"Is he okay now?"

"I hope so."

"I'm afraid my affairs are hammering on Dad's heart."

"No such thing, Jonathan."

But a letter from home sent me hurrying back to Marsley Falls. "Dear Jonathan," my mother wrote. "Fern visits us nearly every day. I could drive her over to Minitown to spend a Sunday afternoon. We both miss you." I sure didn't want any visitors here. I went home.

First I dropped by Fern's to talk to her before my folks could put us through another dinner-table command performance. I had been wondering if maybe she knows more about me than I think. We hiked about a mile out of town to a hilly place where we once picnicked when we were kids. Standing on a hill made me feel strong. I put my arm around her waist. She relaxed and leaned her head on my shoulder. Her voice went soft. "Jonathan, late fall is my favorite time of year. Leaves turn red-gold, brown and yellow. The air gives a hint of winter. It's good to be here with you, warm and snug together." She sounded kind of, like, rehearsed to me. Not like the Fern I've always known. However, it was good to daydream about falling in love with her. She looked great, also like she needed me.

We sat down on a bed of leaves. She picked strands of browning grass, wove a braid, then tossed it away. I wondered what to do. I thought of giving her my high school ring. Maybe it might set things right, like we could be engaged while I went away to college. She'd meet someone else. Things could be solved that way. Suppose she really could save me from being myself? Better yet. I drew her closer, kissed her shoulder where the sweater had slipped down. Her arms went around my neck. She touched my face with her lips. It felt fine, like when my mother used to stroke my cheek good night. I covered Fern's lips with kisses. I wanted to give myself the chance to try and make her happy—make us happy.

"Fern, I need you. I care about you."

She pulled away, moved away, and straightened her sweater. A tear rolled down one cheek. She refused my handkerchief and rubbed her face with her bare hand. "Don't give it another try, Jon. You're what you are and I'm who I am. You can't care any more than you do, and no one can make you care. It can't be done. And I can't go on caring—alone."

"You're the closest girl in my life, Fern."

"*Close* only means we're friends."

"Look, there's something I want to confess."

"Jon, save confessions for someone you love."

"Fern, I love you very much."

"Jonathan, I love you completely. I don't even want to qualify it with a 'very much.'"

"But you don't know—"

"I do know, and have been trying not to see it. You like males, not females. You can't help it, I guess."

"How long have you known?" I asked.

"Well, I've been waiting for you to find yourself for two or three years."

"Fern, please let's not break up. I couldn't stand it."

She said, "I betcha one thing, if I were a lesbian and you were straight, you wouldn't give me as much time as I've put in on you and your 'problem.' No, you would not, because males are more selfish, even when they're gay. There's the male part forever taking over."

"You don't want to see me again, Fern?"

"In a while. But not just yet—my friend. Tell your mom to ease up on the dinner invitations—I have to study and . . ."

"I understand."

Dad and Mom were like their own selves again. Some of the strain was gone. Sitting in the living room watching football on TV, thumbing through the Sunday papers, shaking our heads over the state of the world and roasting marshmallows on a stick in a crackling fireplace, all that took me back to being a boy, just a kid with his mother and father—like, back to Turnabout Mountain.

I broke the news about Fern clearly and directly. "Hey, Mom, Fern doesn't care to be my beard anymore."

She snapped to attention. "Whatever is a beard, Jonathan?"

I took a deep breath, popped another marshmallow on a stick and held forth. "Beards have been used as disguises in detective stories, right? Well some gay guys escort girls places, like to dances, bars, *family dinners* and so forth. They do this in order to pass themselves off as straight. Well, the girl is the guy's beard. She's his disguise, got it?"

Mom tried to laugh but didn't manage more than a grimace. "Jon, I don't think you fully realize how deeply Fern cares."

My marshmallow burned and caught fire while I searched for some right words. "If I had a sister—well, I mean if you and Dad had a daughter, would you want her to marry a gay guy in order to try and straighten him out?"

"No. But in your case . . ."

"Mom, there's no but about it. The answer is no. No is the right answer."

Dad jumped in, "Jon, try this one out. If you had a child, would you want that child to be gay?"

A tough question and it sure hurt me to answer. "No way, Dad, it's too hard. But what we want has little to do with what we get. Maybe when you have a child he or she is not your property. A human being can't belong to somebody else forever, not even to parents or lovers.

Someday we're off on our own. Some folks were raised right and are now serving time in jail. Others were raised wrong, in some lousy ghetto, and somehow made it through hell to a happy ending. Dad, we never even got around to building that Lincoln fence on Turnabout Mountain. We meant to, right? Whoever I am, that's how it is. We're doing the best we can."

Mom reached over and touched the top of my head. A welcome touch. "Jonathan, Dad and I have been hearing about a group called Parents of Gays. They hold educational sessions. A friend of mine—well, her sister attends one. They help the parent to understand."

I said, "Do you truly want to do that?"

"Well, not really."

"Then don't. I'm not enrolled in a group to find out what you and Dad are feeling. Let's drop it for a while."

Mom said, "Well, we just might visit that group anyway—at least once."

I burned another marshmallow. We laughed about that. Home felt better. I hated to go back to Minitown.

16 Tyrone Tate

MY FATHER HAS ALMOST PATTED A HOLE IN MY back saying how proud he is of me fitting into the Minitown school. Susan just rolls her eyes and gives me a hard time. "Goody, goody for a fit-in named Tyrone." When Barnett made Theodora Lynn my compu-partner, that bugged Susan to the bone. She made a big noise. "Barnett threw a black boy and a white girl together so they could parade themselves in front of the black girl standing there all by her partnerless self."

"Aw, Sis, come on, you and I do our homework together every night."

"That's not the point."

"Susie, we're the only blacks in school. Who else could he team me with but a white student?"

"He could have put you with a white *boy*, or with me, your sister. I don't want to be your partner. But that's better than me not having one! I'm the odd number."

"Oh, that would look dumb. To have your sister for a partner."

"Ty, those girls in school pass me by like a cold wind, with a breezy 'hi.' They don't even give me time to answer 'hi' back. My own family acts like I'm imagining whatever happens to me."

She's right. Dad's favorite song is how race doesn't really matter. And yet, he can't stand Theo's father because Theo's father can't stand him. But I guess race has nothing to do with *anything.* That's why he doesn't want us to defend Theo. Doesn't make sense.

Mr. and Mrs. Lynn don't often speak to us. They only nod. Mr. Lynn is the main one, tries to pretend he doesn't see us and sweeps his yard with his back turned to our house. But he sneaks a peek over his shoulder. When one of us catches him looking our way he nods real fast and coughs as if that's why he can't talk. Theo and her mother speak to us when he's not around. Mrs. Lynn once told Mom how to find the supermarket. Back where we came from, in Crown Heights, some neighbors talk to new people. They drop by and might bring a pie to say welcome. It bothers me to see my mother wait till the Lynns are not around before she leaves the house. Me, I go and come whenever. After all, too much staying out of the way can wreck your nerves. People who always nod and never speak—they could also get a neck sprain.

In our basement playroom we have a full-size pool table that came with the house. We have a bar and an old-time jukebox, also came with the house. The box lights up like a big-deal game machine. A fine sound. We put in nickels for it to play old 78-RPM records. You can get back your nickels from the back of the box. Uncle Kwame gave me most of his record collection. He got a lot of them from old people who dig him. My father no longer spins Ruth Brown, Eckstine, Rushing and Count Basie; not even Billie Holiday singing a collector's favorite, "Strange Fruit." Dad said, "Play that music low or white folks around here might think we're common." Neat music like that is uncommon, I say. My father seems scared to enjoy himself since he's been a success in the mainstream. We don't joke much and he doesn't even talk black anymore. He's quit calling his people "the brothers and the sisters." He's trying to get *accepted* by the power structure, that's what Uncle Kwame says.

Well, my mother sure is accepted. She says she's overaccepted. White folks send her invites to join the school board, PTA, the nonpartisan political association, and big-time disease outfits like Cancer Aware and Heart Watch. Uncle Kwame says, "Of course, most organizations want *one* of us. But only *one.* Sometimes they'll strain themselves and take in two. They're looking for *predictable Negroes*. They like to know our thoughts in advance. But even if they do make a mistake on mind reading your mama ahead of time, what can they lose? They got her outvoted. Believe me, each and every meeting she attends has been held before she arrives. Yeah, the night before, by telephone. They know what they're going to vote on, who will make the motion, who's to second it and just about how many will vote yea or nay. And their words are nicely framed so as to also take you in and capture your one vote. Then meeting can be adjourned, all fair and square."

Dad shook his head and raised his hands, like, giving up on his brother. "Kwame, you're so angry behind that smile. I don't know what to do with you."

My uncle slapped his hands together and stomped his feet, cracking up over his own wise wisdom. "Max, here's some advice. Just do the same with me as you do with these crackers who are trying to drive you crazy and run your tail out of town and off into the sunset. Just keep saying howdy-do and looking pleasant."

He lolled back in the leather armchair and went on needling us about living in a white neighborhood. But he is here with us, and my father didn't even have to send for him. Their older sister, Aunt Lovey, that's what we call her—she phoned and told Uncle Kwame, "Someone tried to burn our brother's house." And Dad had told her first because he knew she would tell Uncle Kwame. He takes a roundabout way to do some things.

Uncle Kwame is a good looking, almost jet-black man, I'd say. He's shorter than Dad and twice as tough. He was hanging loose, all relaxed with one leg over the arm of our newest lounge chair. My mother doesn't let us do that. But she's not going to bug my uncle 'cause she's so glad to see him. He and my father look almost like twins. I mean, quins—Uncle Kwame says down-home country folks say quins when they mean twins. So that's why he says it, to be like them. My father says, "But you know better, man. They also say *two quins* when they're talking about one set of twins. That'd be *ten* people. *Quins* stands for *quintuplets*, which means five. So two quins—"

Uncle Kwame likes to have a good time, even in the middle of a war—so he said, "I wonder if some *quins* burned that damned cross on your lawn last night? Quins, twins, triplets or one lone night rider, the result is all the same."

My father was polishing his legal rifle. Uncle Kwame was checking out a handgun between sips of apple juice. Dad said, "Brother, where did you get that?"

"None of your business, Max."

Mom stopped smiling. "Look, fellows, don't make things worse. Put away the guns before one goes off and you both land in jail. Whoever burned that cross is not going to show up to claim credit. More likely you'll make a mistake and shoot the mailman or the garbage collector." My father put the rifle back on the wall as Mom went on. "At least Max belongs to a rifle club. But Kwame, do you have a license for a handgun?"

My uncle said, "Lady, did the perpetrator have a cross-burning license? Anyway, I still bet your next-door neighbor *could* be the one who did it, or at least knows where it came from. On the other hand," Uncle Kwame winked one eye shut while going into deep thought, "it's not likely he did it. The wind *could* have shifted and his house truly might have been burned along with yours. Someone at a distance had a hand in it, and the reason Lynn declared his innocence is because of his daughter's troubles. He sure doesn't need one more."

The burning cross had licked up one side of our house and left it burned black. On the way in, that next afternoon, Uncle Kwame snatched Dad's new sign off the lawn, "Beware of the dog." He spray painted another sign on the back, "Beware of the man." First thing he said was, "Don't expect a dog to do what a man won't do for himself. Protect your own premises. You don't even own a damn dog."

I feel better with Uncle Kwame and Dad taking time off to stay home with us. But I'm going to school. No need for me to hide. After all, that might make the cross burner feel good.

A couple of weeks ago Theodora came over to our house while her parents were out. She wanted to practice making a divided screen on the computer monitor and working two files at the same time. Later, Mom came down, with Mr. Lynn behind her. He said, "Theo, get up and come home."

After they left, my mother lit into me. "It did not look nice for you to entertain that white girl in our basement." She said basement like it was a sinful place.

"Ma, the computer is in the *playroom*—which is also the basement."

"You know her father doesn't like us, so don't bring her in here at all."

"I didn't bring her."

"She has a very questionable reputation."

"What did she do?"

"Oh, people hint things about her."

"Like what?"

"Never you mind, Tyrone. Just don't let her in the house again, even if she asks."

"That would be rude."

"Do it nicely."

So this is life in the mainstream. It's like a fast video. Okay . . . I'll keep Theodora Lynn out of the house and avoid Jonathan Barnett.

17 *Mrs. Mitchell*

IN MY YEARS AS PRINCIPAL I'VE SHAPED THIS school. A part of me is invested in every child, parent and teacher that passes through our doors. I work hard to bring in the new and preserve the best of the old in our classrooms. I've tried to make an institution into a pleasant public home. Over our entrance, at the top level of the granite stairway, above solid oak doors, are the words "Welcome to Minitown High School." A mosaic of stones glinting gold, white and blue.

The beautiful strength of this old building gives me courage to face a world fast turning into chrome and concrete. We still have leather chairs in our offices and solid brass door locks. For twenty-two years, as teacher and principal, I've worked to maintain the image of a good, strong, dependable school. We still have hedges, shrubbery and evergreens, in spite of bouts with now-and-then vandalism by spray painters. I didn't look for guilty parties. Everyone had to skip one favorite class period and help clean up the mess. Vandalism stopped. I stemmed the tide of destruction and kept fairly calm while doing it. The fight for academic survival should look as graceful and elegant as possible, especially when it's in the hands of a woman.

The youngsters call me *Mitch* when they think I'm out of earshot. Sounds tough, but I understand. Young people crave adult targets. I've been on this earth over fifty years, so I know a little about life. Daily living is a very personal challenge. Being a woman leader is quite tricky. In the morning, while dressing, I also put on a wise look to help me through the day. At night I take it off. Once in a while I cry secretly. It's not easy to work this hard job.

Everybody thinks I'm made of indestructible stock. That's frequently expressed as admiration from a teacher. "Well, Mrs. Mitchell, fortunately nothing gets you down." Little do they know. Even maintaining the right image in this school calls for constant effort, right down to what I wear as opposed to what I *want* to wear. Not a thing in my closet really pleases me. I'm stocked with well-cut jackets and skirts and softly colored flowered and fruit-print dresses and blouses, trying to look tailored and feminine all at once. I'd really like to come to school in a red flowing chiffon gown and a garden hat, or how about shocking pink slacks and a traffic-light-green blouse? The best dream of all, a gold-sequined bikini that dares not go near the water. But I, like most sensible people, learn how not to do any and everything I want to do if it interferes with work. I make it my business to look conservatively chic, with barely a hint of daring. A strawberry-print scarf or my green ceramic earrings. I can't allow myself to shock others. But nothing is supposed to shock me. There's not a thing happening now that hasn't happened before, nothing new under the sun. It's how we take it—that's what counts.

Right now, unfortunately, all I have room to think about is sexual controversy, rape, incest, child molestation, homosexuality—and AIDS prevention discussions. Such subjects can drive a school board and the PTA to the brink of madness. Newspapers, motion pictures, magazines, books and television all give daily accounts of the latest hot kinks. Children and adults tune in every evening to hear and see the latest murders and sexual news of the day. The family that hears together all too often leers together. Well, two hoorays for all-out freedom. I'm withholding one because some of the same parents who watch with the kiddies don't want to hear that any of those ideas are being analyzed in school. That *shocks* 'em.

Sexual ignorance abides in the house of education. Young and old are dancing to deafening, monotonous, electric rock music. Shaking their back and front sides in time to the most sexually explicit music in the world. But we, in the educational system, risk our professional lives to bring up a decent, serious sex discussion in a classroom. Most students seem to think that nothing sexual took place before they were born. Their own lifespan is the beginning and end of all existence. Eternity is dead history behind them—or part of a future that will never show up. Everything beyond their own moment is simply nonexistent. Well, certain "honest" people in this school are about to wake us up in a rather rough, sudden way. The fools in our younger generation think older heads never heard of offbeat lifestyles.

When I was a child my family used to visit Aunt Ida Ray, my father's sister. That was not her original name. My parents said her name was first Wilfred, then Clayton and finally she changed it to Ray. Once, childlike, I barged into Auntie's business. "Why did you change your name, Aunt Ida?"

"Well," she said, "I was married once and that changed it. Then I became unmarried."

"You were divorced?"

"That's right. When a woman marries, she changes her name. However, when a boy is born he remains himself. If he marries he remains the same person. He is John Brown forever, unless he just doesn't like that name and decides to legally select another. Well, I decided to choose a name for myself. I also divorced my original family ties along with the husband, and decided to claim a fresh, new name, in hopes that I'd forever know who I am."

"Oh. And now you always know?"

"Well, most of the time. But echoes from those maiden and marriage names still whirl around in my head."

"Oh, you are strange, Aunt Ida."

"Thank you, child."

I had not meant it as a compliment, but she graciously

took it that way. She had wavy brown hair with gray streaks. At that time she must have been about thirty-eight. I considered that quite old.

She lived with a lady named Miss Ellen who was even older. They seemed very content and had a small cozy house full of pleasant things, like China lamps and jars of homemade strawberry-ginger jam. There was a big shiny ornate brass bed that had once belonged to Miss Ellen's grandparents. They also had a backyard. It was not a patio or a terrace, it was a genuine yard. There was a swing out there. Vegetables as well as flowers. Aunt Ida always picked a bouquet for me to take home. She also gave us a jar of jam with a layer of wax under the lid.

Miss Ellen owned a fancy cut-glass stemmed bowl filled with sugared candy. The candy was brightly colored and shaped like orange slices and green leaves. The sparkly jar stood on a small round mahogany table. Miss Ellen let me lift the lid and make my own selections. One time I dropped it and chipped the ball on top of the cover. She soothed me and stopped Mama and Papa from scolding. "But things are to be used. It's far better for cut glass to show a chip than never to be handled at all. People are also like that. There's a saying—It's better to have loved and lost, than never to have loved at all. But we may get a chip or a nick now and then."

"Now it's worth less than before." Mama was upset. Miss Ellen remained calm about the breakage.

"Well, we never planned to sell it, so it hasn't lost value. Right here is where our chipped jar will remain—the cracked reminder of a very happy day."

After we left, my parents spoke in hushed tones about how good it made them feel to have visited *them*.

Over the years they often remarked about Ida Ray and Miss Ellen being "that way" about each other. They talked about how *discreetly* the "girls" handled their *arrangement*. Such remarks were always followed by a headshake, a sigh, or a little nervous laughter. Many years later I realized that Aunt Ida and Miss Ellen were lesbians.

In our church there was an organist. He held his head very high and played beautifully. I recalled hearing a few nervous snickery remarks about him. "He's sort of swishy, but awfully talented—and just as *nice* as he can be." That's the way it was. People didn't hold open discussions about delicate matters. Life was allowed to proceed peacefully.

In my younger years others seemed more discreet on either side of every fence. There was a lot of polite looking the other way . . . and Aunt Ida Ray, Miss Ellen and the organist didn't try to beat everyone to death about their situations. Now there's entirely too much discussion about personal matters. Some things ought to remain behind closed doors.

I will not allow Jonathan Barnett to foolishly run his honest mouth before a school board to damn himself in order to save others. The poor boy is willing to throw away his future and interfere with ours. Mini High must not be turned into a war zone.

I forced myself to do an unethical thing. I invited him to my home . . . to privately put him on the right path.

Along with dinner, I fed him a few of the old clichés that still make solid sense—Let sleeping dogs lie. All's well that ends well. Don't bother trouble unless trouble bothers you. Mainly I pointed out, things that *almost* happen have not happened at all. Take for example such slippery subjects as *attempted* rape, *threatened* blackmail, the *anonymous* burning of a cross on the lawn of a black family. A delinquent girl's *alleged* accusations against a teacher who's a star member of the community. How lucky we are that there are words such as *almost* and *alleged*. *Almost* gives everybody another chance.

Dinner was an uncomfortable time, because I care about all concerned. However, I'm particularly worried about poor Rex Hardy. A few years ago he came to Minitown with a small cloud over his head. He did honestly discuss it with me. It seems that a girl in a summer camp briefly had him in court on a charge of molestation. She was fourteen, a minor. Hardy was judged innocent. Absolutely not guilty. I wish he had not told me about it. He could have kept his mouth shut once he was found innocent. Repeating that kind of story leaves an ugly echo in the air. A "not guilty" decision does not help your case when the same charge is made against you the second time.

I invited Jonathan Barnett to dinner so we could one-to-one things in a relaxed atmosphere. I clearly explained that I don't believe Theodora Lynn's parents want to make a public scene about this. Hardy certainly doesn't. After all, he has a fine family, a dear wife and two lovely children. They could be destroyed by the

Lynn story. "Now, Jonathan," I said, "there's also that black family. The Tates don't care to have Tyrone involved. There's enough on their minds trying to get over a cross burning. I suggest you bow out of attending the school board meeting. You can go home to visit your family or something."

"Mrs. Mitchell," he said, "I didn't ask to attend the board meeting. The board *invited* me. All I'll do is answer their questions."

"We don't need a court case in a schoolroom meeting," I reminded him.

"Yes, ma'am. But I'm receiving anonymous phone calls, and mean notes in my mailbox—threats. 'Barnett, don't speak to the school board or the whole town will be told you are a faggot.'"

"Well, my dear, you just deny that ugly rumor and I'll stand by you. We have wonderful board members. They've received the same notes. They're not interested. They regard them as malicious lies against you."

Then came the surprise. Barnett looked me right in the eye and foolishly said, "It's not a lie. I *am* gay."

I'm sure he thought he was telling the truth. But truth, like a diamond, has many facets. A dinner talk with a headstrong young man is no June picnic. I wanted to shake him until his teeth rattled. He sat there slowly and deliberately picking brandied walnuts out of my Granger Bakery's nine-dollars-a-pound deluxe spice cake.

"Young man, do you need your name and face on television about this kind of thing?"

"No, I don't, Mrs. Mitchell. My parents don't need it either."

"Well, stop being so stubborn."

"How am I being stubborn?"

"You did not see what you thought you saw! Now, would you care for some coffee?"

"No thanks. And I know what I saw."

"Couldn't you possibly be mistaken? Did you *see* Mr. Hardy tear her clothing? Did he actually have his hands on her?" I lit into him good. "Life is not laid out simply, like ABC's. It's complicated." I didn't mean to shout, but the boy's head is a hard stone to crack. "Look, son, Mr. Hardy attends the same church as the Lynns. And their pastor is an alternate school board member. That's a touchy situation. Do you know that Rex Hardy even helped your landlady, Mrs. Trale? He told her when that house was coming up for sale. He also got her to post the studio apartment for faculty rental. Thanks to him you're living there."

He pushed his cake plate to one side and sassed me. "What have I to do with all that?"

"Nothing at all, boy. All you have to do is look out for yourself, then take off for college or home or wherever you want to go. That's all you have to do."

He *wanted* to give in—"Okay," he said. "I'm *not* gay. All I'm saying is I saw what I saw."

I made one more plea for reason. "Jonathan, perhaps she tore her own clothing. Certain girls sometimes do things like that."

He shook his head as if he felt sorry for me. "Mrs.

Mitchell, I don't believe Theodora did that. Why do you and the board want me to call her a liar?"

I was on my feet slamming my fist against the table. "Don't pull that holier than thou act on me! I'm thinking of Hardy's wife and children. I'm looking out for Theodora's future."

I felt my face going into a deep red blush. Yes, I was ashamed of asking this child to keep quiet to avoid a scandal, to ease us all out of a tight squeeze. Why was I begging him to save that silly Hardy when my natural sympathy is with Theodora, the *almost* victim? I'd like to run that stupid gym teacher out of town with a horse whip. But it's still my school. What good is a moment of truth if the institution suffers more than the guilty? If Rex Hardy was anywhere other than where he is, I'd go against him. He *is* too damned free with his hands. Patting and pinching the girls is not called for at all. No, I don't believe Theodora's lying. I wish three troublesome people would get out of my life: Hardy, Theo and this boy Barnett. Then I could deal with normal everyday difficult problems.

I made another last try. "Our board members might ask why you and Tyrone Tate were playing in the gym during class time."

"I was waiting to start class," he said. "Mr. Hardy told me you had given permission to rehearse cheerleaders during my period."

"Well, if you do show up at the board meeting, don't make any declarations about sexual preferences. The school board does not care to hear that from you or anyone else." My voice had gone high soprano. I was out of control. "You do not have to explain or deny anything *personal.*"

"It seems to me, Mrs. Mitchell," he said, "heterosexual or homosexual is not the question. What about Theodora Lynn? Why should I back off because of sexual accusations? We are who we are."

Perhaps thinking of him as "child" or "boy" was an error. "Jonathan, what about *you*? Forget confessions. Let the world of anonymous callers say what they will. Learn to stand strong and *silent.* Anonymous people deserve no truth. Believe me, at seventeen you don't yet know enough about yourself to declare anything."

He looked worried. Kept rubbing one foot into my oriental rug. Hard enough to wear down the nap. "Mrs. Mitchell, I just don't like other people making declarations for me, by mail or phone."

"Then if you don't want others to speak against you, why speak against yourself?"

"It would be different coming from me. And I'd never feel threatened by anyone again. At least it wouldn't matter as much. Whoever, whatever I am has nothing to do with the situation."

I changed that dangerous subject. "Jonathan, she might listen to you. Ask Theodora to drop the *attempted* rape accusation. She hasn't been actually harmed physically."

"She could have been harmed in other ways. She's a child."

"Yes, but she has some very womanish, forward ways."

"Mr. Hardy is an adult, he has forward ways too. But

he ought to know better. A child should be safe with an adult. Anyway, thanks for dinner, Mrs. Mitchell."

"Oh, you didn't care for your spice cake?"

"Yeah, sure. It was great. Also the chicken."

So I had failed all around. We'd had veal scallopini. I hadn't reached him at all. He's awfully young to look so tired.

"Mr. Barnett, do you have the disks and notes which Theodora said she left on top of her computer?"

"No, I haven't."

"If you come across them, will you give them to me?"

"I don't know—but—oh, sure, why not?"

Well, I felt better. Never say die.

18 Kwame Tate

WHAT AM I DOING IN A TOWN WHERE NOT another man looks like me, except my brother Max? In the past we've locked horns about differences of opinion. But nobody in this place, or any other, is going to burn him down while I stand by doing nothing but finding fault with his ways. Ways or no ways, he's my brother. When it comes to cross burning I get the burners' fiery message like it's being sent to me personally. They're talking to me, even if the fire is a thousand miles away. The flames shout, "Hey, Kwame, this is for you too."

Nobody likes to say or hear "I told you so." But one is now in order. I told Max not to move out here with these strange people. Being the only one of anything, anywhere, is unnatural. Who needs to be the only zebra in a pride of lions? So why did he do it? He's jumping into the middle of what he calls the American mainstream. "So go on," I said, "leap, brother, leap. But watch your back." He's making more money than most of us. And there's lots of good things for money to do. But I have never seen a dedicated money-maker who didn't need much more than the plenty he was making. All they see, smell and think about is how to touch another dollar. They get carried away with the idea, and soon their noses are chained to a money grindstone.

Max is busy working his way back into *slavery*. But this time on a comfortable level. Lately he's been overusing a few popular words and phrases like "lifestyle," "image" and "crossover," and "the way the game is played," and it's "all about making a buck." I told him that when the bottom falls out of the black community, he's going to get sucked down the big hole with everybody else. If he thinks he can ignore the rest, and let poor folks go under while he rises higher, he's got another think coming.

One Sunday afternoon, back in Crown Heights, Max stood in my backyard and hollered, "Why don't *your* people stop committing crimes? Maybe they just might find some kind of job." When he moved on up a little higher, the rest of the race became *your* people. Mine, not his.

I took him in the house before somebody passing by might hear him and think it was me spreading ignorance. I sat my brother down beside the bag of golf clubs he had parked in my kitchen on his way to drive twenty miles out of town, on his way to the links. "Look, man," I said. "There are babies being born this minute who will never ever get a job in life. Their looks won't clear with certain people. Just being who they are might not please the job givers. And we can't run folks' business, right? Fairness by law is too undemocratic, okay? It's their business, so they hire who they want. But some can't find a job and that's a fact. And a lot may not be as smart or as lucky as you. But a job is a butt-certain necessity. Everybody working is to your advantage, dummy. A job for everybody makes for a peaceful neighborhood. The jobs ain't there. Those that are have no merit badge. We got full-time jobs that don't pay enough to meet the rent money, to pay for groceries and carfare to work. That's why you have to be concerned about other people besides yourself." He looked at me from under his designer golf cap. Looked bewildered, worried, mad and pitiful. I wondered how we grew up in the same house, with the same parents and got to thinking so differently about things. Once, he had the nerve to tell me, "Mama must have been frightened by a radical Harlem street speaker while she was carrying you."

Well that was then and now is now. What am I doing walking along in this weird Minitown on a dark night, computer disks in my pocket, looking for a queer white boy who lives on Beamer Street? In Manhattan, back in understandable New York City, most every street has a number. You know that if you're on 125th Street, the next one will be 126th. Numbers move along sensibly, one by one. So you know in which direction to run. But who can tell where Beamer Street might be? You have to know the mean town in order to find any place in it. Well, as they say, when you leave New York you ain't goin' nowhere.

I passed a white woman a few blocks ago. She hurried to the other side of the street, looking scared of me. Well, all she sees of my likeness is on her nightly TV crime reports. Good thing she didn't scream. I'd be in deep trouble, or dead. At the very least I'd be open to police questions. "Do you live around here?" "Where are you going?" "Where are you from?" Okay, so what the hell am I doing here? "Well, police officer, I'm looking for a seventeen-year-old white misfit named *Mr.* Jonathan Barnett." Guess it's okay to admit I'm kinda scared. Max always thought I was fearless from childhood on up. One time he called on me to save him from a big bad bully. The kind who was known to carry brass knucks, a blade *and* a gun. I bravely saved Max and myself while scared blue. I wasn't bluffing. But I guess a bully knows when he meets somebody willing to die. Well, not willing, just ready. It goes right through me these days to see so many good folks scared to speak up against wrong.

Now, Tyrone, he hangs in like tough and fearless. But I don't like how hard headed he's moving. The kid's after making himself a public target. Maybe his mom was frightened by a ten-ton stone while carrying him. Ty is stubborn.

After the fire my brother got several mean offers to buy their new house. But the buyers are mainly willing to just take over his mortgage. Real estate hawks know how to move on in and make money out of racial hot-spot zones. However, it's not that easy to run away. Where can we run?

Yesterday we went, Max and I, to try and see Jonathan Barnett and Mrs. Mitchell. The high school principal told us that couldn't be done. She kept looking down at her desk, up at the ceiling and back down to studying her wristwatch. Then she flipped through a book to let us know she was thinking of an appointment. Everything in that school is neat, clean and polished to a fine shine. But their minds are rusty.

Mrs. Mitchell also told us the gym teacher was absent and unavailable. Max tried to explain, "Racists are making anonymous threats because it seems they fear Tyrone will serve as a witness against this Mr. Hardy." You'd think someone had goosed her every time we called Hardy's name.

"Really, Mr. Tate, as far as we know there's been nothing to witness, in a way of speaking, at least up to this point."

Hey, now examine that statement with a magnifying glass and you'll make no kind of sense out of it. I told her, "What we want is for all concerned to know that the Tate family doesn't want any part of white folks' business."

Max shook his head, warning me to drop any mention of race, and said, "Race has nothing much to do with it."

She grabbed at that straw. "You're right, Mr. Tate, race has nothing at all to do with anything in this school as far as I know." The lady is full of self-protective qualifying sentences. She really can shadowbox and spar with words.

"Mrs. Mitchell, could we please speak to Mr. Barnett, the computer instructor?"

She nixed that. "He's *not* available."

We thought it best to give up on her.

Jonathan Barnett is also white, but he's a young outsider, so I guess he doesn't count for much in this small-time power structure. Well, that evening I had one last good talk with Tyrone and got nowhere. "Boy, why should you care about any of 'em, particularly that Theodora trash who lives next door?"

"I don't," he said.

"Well then, forget about what you think you saw."

"Uncle Kwame, I haven't talked to anybody. I won't unless I'm asked—as a witness in court."

"Tyrone, why can't you just say you didn't see anything? Say it *now*. And save those next-door folks the trouble of going to court."

"Oh, I don't want to lie like that, Uncle Kwame."

"Tell me this, do you think the Lynns could lie about you?"

"Maybe they would."

We were down in the basement. Ty was practicing pool shots at the billiard table. A green-shaded ceiling lamp threw a yellow circle of light over his head. Susie was chalking cue sticks. Both faces were strained, worried.

I looked around that fine family playroom. A pool table, a computer and printer, remote-control TV, video recorder, an exercise mat and weights, a punching bag. Better than anything my brother Max and I had when we were tenement kids. Damn, his children have everything but peace of mind. In one corner of the room is a freezer full of food. Steaks, shrimp, all kinds of expensive goodies. When I was a youngster we were lucky to be able to play kick the can down the street and get mealy franks and beans for supper.

"Hey, Tyrone, as I was saying—"

"Uncle Kwame, I'm not offering either to tell or to run away from telling what I saw, okay?"

"Boy, what's this with you and a sudden big desire to tell the truth about other people's business?"

"Well, I'm not scared, for one thing, not afraid of white people like you and Dad are."

Oh, I had to pull Max off him, and Max is gentle. The boy made him so mad till tears ran down his father's face. "I'll kill him!" Sister-in-law and niece had to jump in front of Ty to protect him from his daddy. The luxury house was jumping. Max stomped across the floor, picked up the computer disks and waved them in the air. "Boy, I'll take this mess out in the backyard and burn them. That will be the end of the so-called evidence."

I said, "Look, brother, one fire out there was one too many." Max didn't carry out his threat. I got Barnett's phone number from the phone company and set up an appointment.

So here I am, a dark man on a dark block, standing under one weak street lamp in front of a stranger's suburban house on a very dark night. I opened the gate.

A white woman raised a second-story window. "Who's there?"

"I'm looking for Mr. Barnett."

The porch light flipped on and she gasped at the sight of me, then said nervously, "Follow the path around to the back entrance. Well, well, well!"

"I am Kwame Tate, Tyrone's uncle." At last, finally face to face with Jonathan Barnett, I placed the disks and the grubby notes on the center of the table between us. He looked sorry to see them, but was quick on the pickup.

"Yes, Theo said there was missing evidence to prove her story."

"Yeah," I said, "and here it is, Jack."

"May I ask where you got it?"

"Well, let's say it kind of *came* to my attention—it was *brought* to my attention."

"Well, Mr. Tate, why didn't you pass it on to Theo or her parents? Your brother lives right next door."

"Next-door neighbors can be miles apart after crosses are burned. Man, if you're old enough to instruct a class you should be able to handle class business. If the principal trusts you to teach students, well, Tyrone, Theo and Susan gotta trust you to be responsible."

He dropped them on the table. You'd think those disks were red-hot coals. "If you don't want to be bothered—burn the stuff. Burning seems to be a way of life around here."

"Mr. Tate, I've been getting anonymous calls about this crap."

"Yeah," I said, "my brother has a few skunks ringing his phone. Your name keeps coming up. They say you're a faggot and have been hanging out with Ty."

"That's not true," he said. "Ty's no part of my life, believe me."

"Oh, I believe, because I first checked it out with Tyrone. My nephew knows he doesn't have to lie to me. As far as I'm concerned everybody can be themselves as long as they don't hassle me."

"Thanks, Mr. Tate, for bringing the disks."

"No sweat." I split the scene.

After I left, the landlady again let up the front upstairs window, turned on the floodlight and shouted down, "Did you have a good time? Shame on you. This is a fine how do you do! Shame, shame! At least you could stick to your own kind and your own age!"

Windows across the street went up, and other people popped their heads out and called, "What's going on? Need any help over there, Mrs. Trale?" I started to run but was afraid that might get me shot. I could hear my heart beating double time in my eardrums. Why hadn't I asked the kid to walk me to the corner? I couldn't. I made my feet stroll along slowly. Just kept to an easy-going innocent walk. My mouth went dry. Somehow I managed to summon up a low whistle. The tune, I think, was an oldie. "On the Sunny Side of the Street." Hah. And it was pitch dark.

I got home in a cold sweat, but I got there. So much for going out of my way to do Susan, Ty and a white child some kind of a favor. It might have been easier to go next door and hand that evidence to her parents. But the shortest distance is sometimes the longest road to travel.

19 Jonathan Barnett

I HAD THOUGHT OF NOT SHOWING UP, BUT HERE I am, my first time at a school board meeting. Eleven people sitting at a long oak table on gray metal folding chairs. All of them are older than I am, but that's no surprise. Board meetings start with small talk. The members ask about each other's families. Also they give their latest golf scores and ask where did everyone go on their last vacation.

A new person, an outsider like me, is definitely left out, except for the weather. Everybody's in on that. Somebody asked, "Kind of warm for this time of year, wouldn't you say?"

I answered the lady with an instant smile, "Yes indeed ma'am, warm."

Others joined in. "Surprisingly." "One doesn't know how to dress for it." A man in a minister's collar said, "However, it's not really uncomfortable. I'd say it's rather pleasant."

A businessish-looking fellow added, "But we could

stand more crackle and crispness in the air by now. A bigger hint of good football weather."

I tried to stay calm by thinking of the boards I've heard of, board of health, board of directors and parole board. Boards seem to be people who make decisions about other people's business.

After the meeting was called to order by the chairperson, one Mr. Burnham, the board began to close in on me with casual-sounding questions. I gave them a true description of the cleaning closet events about three times. They kept on, gently trying to make me doubt myself. The minister kindly informed me that this meeting was not a trial. Felt like one.

Mrs. Mitchell nervously twisted a curl of mixed gray hair around her index finger and told them what they already knew about Theo's charges. Then she added in a sunny, upbeat tone of voice, "Jonathan Barnett is our *temporary* computer instructor. He's getting promising results in his class." She was wearing a tan dress with little red cherries printed all over it.

Another lady, wearing huge silver rimmed eyeglasses, said, "Oh, good news. I love to hear about promising things."

Wow, being here to discuss a charge of attempted rape, while being blackmailed as a gay—that's too much promise coming from one instructor.

Mrs. Mitchell started again. "Jonathan . . . Mr. Barnett . . ."

"Jonathan is okay, Mrs. Mitchell."

"You do admit you did not clearly see the man's face

when Miss Lynn ran out of that closet?" Her eyes looked steely hard. I believe she likes me okay, but it's just that she *loves* Mini High. To her I must seem like a vulture of disgrace, flapping its funky wings over her fine model school.

"Mrs. Mitchell—his back was kind of turned. Mr. Hardy had fallen to one knee, I guess."

"Oh, then it's difficult to say exactly who it was."

"It was Mr. Hardy."

Mrs. Mitchell kept trying. "This is a serious charge."

"But I haven't charged anybody with anything. Theodora Lynn's making charges, not me."

"Well," said the minister, "why not explain? Tell us what you thought you saw."

Right then a cafeteriaman wearing a white apron and cap rolled in a stainless-steel cart with coffee and danish. Principal Mitchell gladly announced a break.

I skipped coffee and thought about last night, after Kwame Tate had left. Violet Trale, my landlady, came down to ask me for an *extra* month's rent in advance. She rapped on the door and abruptly called out, "Mr. Barnett, your original one month's advance will not be sufficient. Two is more than fair. Anything owed to you will be settled on the day of your departure. Please pay up by tomorrow." Her voice was sharp as an ax.

"Yes, ma'am."

"Also, you did not ask permission to keep a pet. Get rid of it."

"But Mrs. Trale, Lataweeze is *your* cat."

"No such thing. She's a stray without shots. We don't

need to harbor a possible source of rabies or AIDS on my premises."

"AIDS?"

"Yes, sir, Acquired Immune Deficiency. And if you thought it was *my* cat, why did you name her Lataweeze?"

"Oh, Mrs. Trale, it was just a thought."

"Yeah. Some people love to think differently from the rest of us, don't they? Another thing, my young friend, no more night visitors. Particularly *black* ones. It does not look nice to the neighbors, and it shows disrespect for me and my home. If it happens again I'll call the police."

Her footsteps faded away. She went upstairs and paced back and forth. Lataweeze curled against my left leg, purring. I scratched the back of her head. "Don't worry, old girl. Where I go, you go. A stray indeed. You're no more stray than I am." Lataweeze is a fine tabby. Smoky gray with a darker stripe. There's, like, a white bib under her chin and each paw wears a snow-white fur boot. Her eyes are amber with black pupils. Whatever the weather, every evening she waits on the steps to follow me in for the night. She's *friendly*. If anybody gets AIDS it won't be from a cat. Me, I sure would hate to die of AIDS. I'd rather depart from life by way of something "respectable," like tuberculosis or even cancer. I don't want to die of anything ugly. However, maybe it's kind of ugly to die at all. Hell, why shouldn't I, like other people, want to live for a long time?

Lataweeze had stretched forward from the top of her

head back to her hind legs. Then she sauntered to the food bowl, walked around it and gave me a mild meow, like she knew I felt scared and lonely. I served her my one tin of skinless, boneless, Portuguese sardines instead of dry Kat Krunchies. While eating she suddenly stopped to peer over her shoulder, ever on guard against enemies. Always alert and ready to defend herself at all times. Satisfied nothing was stalking to the rear, she finished dinner, napkined her mouth with a furry paw, gave a thank-you turn around my right foot and moved back to her favorite corner. God makes wonderful creatures, especially cats like Lataweeze. It sure is good to have one unquestioning friend. Then and there I made up my mind to come to this board meeting. I couldn't run anymore. Not from threats in the middle of the night or those phone calls. "Nigger lover, faggot, get out of town." "We've written to school board about you and your lovers." "If you don't get out as a witness against Rex Hardy . . ." The same messages over and over. I started picking up on the first ring so as not to further bug my pacing landlady.

In the beginning Mrs. Trale had acted so kind. I used to laugh at her imitations of different townspeople. I recall how one day she came down and brought me what she called a teetotaler mimosa. It was orange juice, ice cubes and seltzer water, served in a long-stemmed fancy glass. "Bubbles without blur, Mr. Barnett," she said. "No sham-pain, got it?" That was when things were friendly.

Just as soon as I put the phone back on the hook, it

rang again. A well-known voice came over loud and clear. "This is Harp. I still owe you a couple of things. One is free advice. Jonathan, drop any talk against Hardy."

"I haven't talked against anybody, Harp."

"I mean at that school board. He's going to defend himself by claiming you are gay."

"How do you know what he's going to do, Harp?"

"Because he called and told me. I guess he did that so I'd tell you."

"Well, Harper Mead, you put me on the end of that pirate's plank, so why does it bother you if he shoves me overboard? I'm ready. I don't care what anybody has to *say* about me or even what they *know* about me. It's coming out time, sink or swim."

"He's about to hint that you and a young black boy have been together too much—the boy is a *minor,* a student."

"He's a liar."

"Okay, but that kind of rumor won't do you any good. Forget the whole messy business. And soothe that hysterical gal."

"Theodora Lynn?"

"Yeah. And if the going gets rough, I'll swear I never told Hardy about us."

"Then you'd be a liar, Harper."

"Hey, Jon, why this sudden, corny yen for truth?"

"Harper Mead, don't you still believe in coming out?"

"Oh sure, to friends, to family, or maybe even the general public, but not to some small-town hick school board or in a silly court case involving a weird little kookie female. Why hang yourself by coming out for the sake of other people?"

"Then why do it at all? It's nobody's business, like I said in the first place, right?"

He sighed. "Listen, coming out is the thing to do when *you're* calling the shots, like saying when, where and how it will be done. Don't go into kicking your soul around for a few square teachers, board members and snot-nosed kids. Why do that to yourself?"

"Because I'm tired of being blackmailed by you and everyone else."

"Come off it, Jon. All I ever demanded was honesty among friends."

"Harper, *demand* sounds like blackmail."

I hung up, took the phone off the hook and left it that way.

Lataweeze brushed against my knee. I reached down and held her close. Something was going on deep inside of her, moving. Hey, she's making kittens. Life goes right on moving no matter who's hurt or ashamed or disgraced or defeated. She's going to have kittens! Whoever and whatever I am, I'm alive too. Life means something good, and I was glad to be a part of it, no matter what. I opened the window. Cool night air swept in. I turned on my music, up, up to *loud,* snapping my fingers to the beat of a hi-fi rocky tune. The landlady stamped on the floor. I laughed and shouted, "Shut up, Violet Trale! We're busy being alive down here." Shouting felt good.

* * *

"Jonathan, Mr. Barnett, we're ready to call the meeting back to order." Now I calmly look around at the Minitown High School Board of Directors. I decide what happens next. I stand up. There's something I want to do—right now. I square back my shoulders and take the icy plunge. Hell, scary truth has got to be better than shivering fear any day. I recall the old Nellie at the "coming out" meeting—Harper's coming out meeting. The old Nellie had said, "You do or don't do your do. And do and say it the way you damned well want it done." Something like that was what he had said. It made sense.

I feel closer to freedom now. It feels good. Chicken Little is about to turn into an eagle. They're all watching and waiting for *me* to speak. The tight place between my shoulder blades relaxes. In front of me, the early evening sun spreads its rosy light beyond the schoolroom window. I place Theo's disks in front of me on the table. I'm ready to do my do that has to be done—coming out.

"Principal Mitchell, school board members, my name is Jonathan Barnett. I am gay. But not at all hilarious about it. The mailman has probably delivered a letter to each one of you—anonymous has been very busy. According to what I saw and heard, I think Rex Hardy attacked Miss Lynn. She said he did and I believe her. I don't plan to talk any more about it, here or anywhere else, unless I'm summoned to court." I feel good. Freedom feels good. "This is the evidence—when needed."

Mrs. Mitchell, tears in her eyes, raises a finger to her

lips trying to silence me but it's too late. Hey, I think maybe she does like me. "Jonathan," she says, "I'm still very certain that you're too young to know exactly who and what you are *yet*."

The minister leans forward. "I request—no, I demand, that this board keep confidential—no, that we *ignore* the statement just made. Mr. Barnett is not on trial here."

"Thank you," I said. "Kindly accept my resignation." Everyone is quiet. You could hear a flea piss on a piece of cotton. It's awfully quiet except for a few sad sighs and a cough. No one asks me to take back my resignation.

The door opens, the office clerk enters and places a note in front of Mrs. Mitchell. She slowly reads it and then shakily announces, "We are notified that according to lawyers on behalf of Miss Theodora Lynn and her parents, and also those representing Mr. Hardy—well, all charges are at least momentarily withdrawn. It is not likely that either party will be returning to this school. In light of the circumstances I'm sure we should all feel somewhat relieved. Mr. Barnett will turn over the disks and let's hope this is the end of the matter." There is a short round of lukewarm applause. I pick up and pocket the disks. "This material is the property of Miss Theodora Lynn. We don't have the right to keep it."

I shake hands all around and say so long. Mrs. Mitchell holds my hand an extra second or two. But no one asks me not to leave . . . they're relieved to see me go. Outside, the evening air bathes my face. Freedom feels great. Coming out is like flying straight up out of this world. Never before have I ever felt this tall. I can't wait to get to my studio to use a phone. I stop at a glass public booth. "Hey, Mom, I'm coming home soon, okay?"

"We'll be looking forward, Jonathan."

"Can you drive over this week and help me move some of my stuff?"

"Whenever you say."

"I say Sunday. Guess what? I have a cat, a female cat."

"What's her name?"

"Lataweeze. She's expecting kittens, okay?"

"Well, you're all welcome."

"How's Dad?"

"Fine. He's asleep."

"Tell him I'm ready to go to college. I'm thinking I need to know—I *want* to know a hell of a lot more than I know right now."

"Jonathan, you sound happy."

"Yeah. What I mean is education could be more wonderful than just passing exams or getting diplomas and degrees. Do you follow what I'm feeling?"

"Yes, I think I do."

"Mom, there's still some part of myself that belongs to me alone, like Dad says. But some things belong to other people. Like, there's maybe an income tax on knowledge. We owe some of it back. A contribution to the source. We shouldn't keep it all for ourselves."

"Can't keep all of our education?"

"Knowledge, I mean."

"Well, that's a fine, generous idea, son."

"Mom, I'm out and doing the best I can with who I am."

"You're a fine person, Jonathan. And I'll be there Sunday to pick you up. You and Cataweeze."

"It's *Lat*aweeze. Sounds like cat, but it's *Lat*."

"Sunday. I'll be there. Shall I ask Fern to come along with me?"

"No, not a soul, Mom."

"All right, I'll be there alone."

Now all I have to do is make a disk delivery to Theodora and let her know I'm still a kindred soul—in case she needs me, in case she changes her mind about the charges against Hardy. I'll also drop by and see the Tates. I don't mind hopping over the Lynn fence.

Last night the TV weather woman said Saturday and Sunday will be bright and sunny. So, suppose it rains? There are four seasons, and I'm going to go through them all, over and over, for as long as I'm able. Someday I look forward to meeting somebody extra-super-special somewhere. If it's a stranger I'll ask a question like "Is it cold enough for you?" Weather is great for openers. Yeah. Rain or shine, if I fly high and hang loose, maybe I'll fall safe.